I0740886

Dedication

for Leslie, Adam, and Sunny

* * *

Acknowledgements

Special thanks to: Leslie Chapin, Edward Kay, Dan Hill, Janice Zawerbny, John Sweet, Beverly Chapin, Michael Levine, Adam Vanderburgh, Daryl Vanderburgh, Jeff Birch and the Small Hope Bay Family, Anne Ramstad, Dan Bodanis, Jay Lang, Matt Crone, Debbie McMahon, John McMahon, Russ Peacock, Zlatko Cetinic, Bill Petrie, Eric Wall, Garth Naumoff, Frank Foley and... Jude Pittman, JD Shipton and the team at BWL Publishing.

Literary Quotation

"I know not with what weapons World War III will be fought, but World War IV will be fought with sticks and stones." Albert Einstein

Careful What You Die For

A.R. Vanderburgh

Print ISBNs
Amazon print 9780228632948
Ingram Spark 9780228632955
Barnes & Noble 9780228632962
BWL Print 9780228632979

BWL Publishing Inc.

Books we love to write …
Authors around the world.

http://bwlpublishing.ca

Copyright 2025 by A. R. Vanderburgh
Editor JD Shipton
Cover artist Pandora Designs

All rights reserved. Without limiting the rights under copyright reserved above, no part of this publication may be reproduced, stored in or introduced into a retrieval system, or transmitted, in any form, or by any means (electronic, mechanical, photocopying, recording, or otherwise) without the prior written permission of both the copyright owner and the publisher of this book. This is a work of fiction. All of the names, characters, places, and events portrayed in this novel either are products of the author's imagination or are used fictitiously. Any resemblance to real or actual events, locales, or persons, living or dead, is entirely coincidental.

Table of Contents

ACT ONE

Chapter 1
Not an Option

Though not a religious man, David Wesson closes his eyes and whispers a prayer. He atones for life regrets and transgressions and offers to put his fate in the hands of a higher power, whatever that may be. He prays that his path be one of righteousness and divine providence.

David checks his air gauge.

A storm of bubbles explodes out of his regulator as he curses his predicament. He's burned through half his air in under fifteen minutes. Above him, a blueish-green crack in a pockmarked coral ceiling leads to the surface, but beyond it, furious, white-streaked waves are thundering onto a glassy ledge. Anyone fool enough to ascend there would be torn to shreds.

David slows his breathing, remembering from this morning's training that at sixty feet below, every nervous breath is the equivalent of three on the surface. He adjusts for neutral buoyancy in the middle of the open cavern, surrounded by stalactites and schools of silvery jackfish. In other circumstances, the sight would be unparalleled in its primordial beauty, but now, it's starting to feel more like a watery tomb.

His mask is almost completely fogged up, but he's too scared to let a controlled amount of seawater in to clear it. Being a novice diver, it's too easy to make a mistake. So he tilts his head forward and swirls the water that is already inside his mask. His view less opaque, David reaches down and sets the direction arrow on his compass. After checking that its magnetic needle isn't being tricked by the metal clasp of his weight belt, he sets off in a westerly direction.

As he swims into the murkiness, David spots a flutter of light. He races toward a coral wall and discovers the source to be a baby sea turtle, its feet flicking and reflecting a ray of ocean filtered sun. David follows the creature's trajectory back with his eyes and voilà: a six-foot-wide opening in the wall. A second baby turtle is struggling to swim out of it.

He all at once remembers that during the briefing there was talk of a turtle sanctuary inshore. This must be it— the passageway he was told to avoid. "It's too easy to get lost in there," they said.

A bit late for that, he thinks.

David switches his headlamp on and starts sculling toward the open mouth. The current is jarringly strong here. He peers into the opening from a distance, and his lamp illuminates a jagged passageway that arcs away and fades to nothingness. He re-checks his pressure gauge.

He can't believe how much air he's burning through, but being a rookie diver, it's hardly a surprise. At least at this shallower depth he can conserve some air.

Visions of family start flooding David's mind. The thought of leaving his beloved four-year-old son fatherless leads him to the conclusion that dying here is not an option. He lets his body slip into a state of acceptance and starts drifting toward the open hollow. David feels the current pushing, then *sucking* him in. His adrenalin surges.

What if it's the wrong way?!

He kicks like an Olympian to reverse course, but it's too late. David tumbles head over fin into the lightless void.

He rockets into the tunnel like he's on some theme-park ride he wished he could get off. He forces his hand up under his chin so the regulator doesn't fly out of his mouth. Without that, *at least it would be over fairly quickly,* he thinks. The thought even relaxes him, until the passage angles sharply downward. David's ears feel like nails are being driven into them. He struggles to equalize their pressure as he plummets.

Forty feet ... Fifty feet ... Sixty feet...

Chapter 2
The Glamourous Life

December 29, 1993
Two days earlier

David Wesson hates Wednesday nights. Playing The Single Malt club with Frankie Sunshine and the Rays is bad enough, but gazing out from under the hot stage lights and watching a half-empty room of seniors devour All You Can Eat Mussels makes David want to crank his bass for the sheer enjoyment of hearing some teacups rattle. At least he'd feel in control for a change.

Club management has already fielded a flurry of complaints that invariably contain three words that crawl like insects under David's skin: "Turn it down!" As far as David is concerned, the louder, the better. Making ears bleed is one of those rare medicines that seems to soothe the savage pain of watching his dreams slip into oblivion. Time for a change he whispers, just like he did exactly one year ago on this very bandstand.

Bandleader Frankie has been around the Miami scene forever. He even played The

Flamingo in Vegas for mobster Bugsy Siegel, or so he says. David, the youngest guy in the band by a longshot, thinks Frankie should have hung up his tired tenor thirty years ago. But bills are bills, and with the unforeseen changes that came into his life so suddenly last year, playing bass with Frankie is a job David can't afford to lose.

To a schooled musician like David Wesson, it's debilitating playing with an ensemble that is so fucking loose. The set list? Oh, what he'd give to be in a "cool" band like Level 42 or Soundgarden. But he sucks it up and refuses to cave, stubborn as a mule in his belief that someday a lightning bolt of luck will strike and change his life forever.

Lounge lizard Frankie, with his jet-black toupee, shirt unbuttoned to the navel and gold chains that brush sensually across his dyed chest hair, insists that the band wear shoulder-padded jackets, pink paisley shirts and skinny ties – a look he thinks is hip. No one has the heart to tell Frankie this is 1993. New Romantic panache faded to oblivion some ten years ago with the death of electropop. At least David has a decent rock mane to counterbalance the trauma of it all.

Halfway through the best song of the night, 'Tie A Yellow Ribbon', David decides to confront drummer Tino about his constant rushing.

"Jeezuz man. Stop speeding up!"

Tino glares at David with murderous eyes.

"Whaddya want, Wesson? A funeral dirge?"

"Seriously man, the original's way slower than—"

Tino and David's heads snap forward.

"Round the ole ... oak... tree," they croon into their mics.

Ronnie Diamond starts honking the melody out of her Baritone Sax while Frankie straightens his coif at a side-stage vanity, lights up a Cuban and shimmies offstage, snapping his fingers on beats one and three. After passing a hippie couple shaking their flower power on the kaleidoscopic dancefloor, Frankie motions for the band to pipe down.

"Where do you folks hail from?" he says, in a Jersey accent that's more pronounced when he's performing. He holds his mic out to a lady seated in a red leatherette swivel-chair.

"We're from London, England" the woman replies in a regal British dialect.

"England?! The land of hope and glory? Lady, at my age, I got more *hope* than glory." Frankie slaps his knee, laughs a little too hard. Tino marks the punchline with a 'ba-dum kssh' drum fill. David sighs.

"And what brings you to Miami, sir? Let me guess ..."

David feels a slow burn rising with every whap of Tino's snare drum.

"There! You're doing it again."

"What's your problem, Wesson? Relax."

"Me relax?"

Tino, distracted by David's pestering, plops out a fill, hitting his stick on the rim in the process, a drummer no-no.

"Round the ole oak ... treeeeeee," the boys sing in perfect harmony as the band slows and ends on a tremulous F6 chord.

The crowd reacts with mild applause.

Frankie hobbles back onstage and dabs his forehead with a monogrammed hankie.

"Thank you, Ladies and Gerbils. Oosh, it's hot up here. Then again, it's always hot when you're with Frankie Sunshine, ladies."

David rolls his eyes, exhausted by years of Frankie's DOA humor.

"Any requests out there? And I don't mean for me to get off the stage. Bwahahaa!"

The audience groans. A couple at the back wave vigorously at the barman for their bill. David uses the opportunity to pound back half a beer from the bottle stashed behind his amp.

"Do you know that one, The Bird Dance?" the British woman shouts. David nearly spits up a mouthful of ale when he hears her request.

"The Bird Dance?! I think we can do that for ya, Princess," Frankie says. "How's about it, boys and girl? Come on up folks, and get ready to flap y'wings!"

David storms to center stage.

"I told you Frankie, no more Bird Dance."

Frankie covers the mic.

"Take it easy, Wesson. What's with you lately?"

"I didn't spend the last fifteen years practicing my fucking instrument... to play this *lounge lizard shit*!"

An awkward hush falls over the room. Frankie looks perplexed momentarily, then flaps his hand at David.

"Folks, I seem to be having some technical difficulties with my bass player. 'The Bored Dance' he calls it. Hah! The kid thinks I need to update m'song list."

"Maybe you should update your toupee while you're at it." David mutters.

"Why you little—"

Frankie lunges at David, grabs him by the lapels and they start grappling with each other, nearly stumbling over the frontstage monitor. Sax player Ronnie rolls her tired eyes. She cues up the delicate composition that surely must have been penned by Mozart.

'Da da da da da da dat. Da da da da da dat. Da da da da dee dee dat Quack Quack Quack Quack.'

Chapter 3
Misty Streets

Miami streets are devoid of people as David ferries Tino home in his rusty '86 Civic.

"That was harsh, dude."

"Tell me about it. It's like that every night."

"No man, I mean the way you treated Frankie. That was uncalled for."

"Nah! Frankie and I are good. It's not the first time we got into a fistfight onstage. Sometimes he even winks and we throw some fake gut punches, but I've never seen him huffing like that."

"Frankie better get his ass to the cardiologist," Tino says. "This is my place up here."

David wheels into the potholed roundabout of Tino's brownstone apartment complex. The musclebound drummer grabs his stick bag and squeezes out of the car.

"So you're not playin' Friday?" he asks on his way out.

"Unfortunately, I gotta sub the one gig a year that actually pays."

"Ouch."

"Family shit."

"Family's everything!"

"I guess so."

"You guess so? Jeezuz, David. Time to snap out of this funk you're in."

"Yeah. You're right, Tino. I'm wound up like a two-dollar watch these days. Anyway, 'til next week. Happy New Year, bro."

"Ah, the glamorous life. Later."

They exchange a secret muso handshake, then David motors off. He picks the tempo up the rest of the way home, the Red Hot Chili Peppers blasting out of custom JBL speakers.

"Give it away, give it away, give it a-way ..." David sings while miming the bass riffs and steering with his knees. He bears left on Northwest First street, where he pulls up in front of his concrete and stucco bungalow and kills the engine.

As he steps out of the car, David takes a moment to relish the quiet of this soon-to-be-developed neighborhood. It's a welcome respite after what's known in the business as a 'hell gig'. He unloads his bass, amp, a worn-out bag of pedals and cords, and grunts the gear up his flagstone walkway, accompanied by the sound of crickets. He glances wistfully at the grassy lot next door, knowing some sleazeball developer will be paving it over next week.

Progress. Yeah right, he thinks.

David ascends the crooked stairs to his front porch, but as he sets his amp down, he's startled by a sharp crunching sound under it. He looks down and sees shards of glass scattered across the landing, glinting under the porch light. He darts his head up and spots a jagged hole in the narrow pane beside his front entranceway. His screen door is bent, half open. The front door, wide open.

"No way!"

David charges into his house.

"Fuuck!"

Chapter 4
A Curious Gathering

A wisp of smoke rises from the smoldering tip of a soldering iron, filling David Wesson's room with a sickly-sweet metallic odor.

"No, you're right. It could have been worse." David glances toward the front of his house. "But they took one of my favorite basses," he sighs. "Hmm? Yes, you did know I play the bass, Ma. Anyway, gotta go. Love you."

David presses End Call and collapses the antenna of his cordless phone. He swings his chair around and faces a goateed man with wire-rimmed glasses seated across the workbench from him.

"Sorry about that."

Surrounded by a clutter of electronic tools and devices, David looks down at a dusty synthesizer that is splayed open atop his work bench. His gaze narrows, then he reaches in and pops out a tiny circuit board. Holding the delicate component between his thumb and forefinger with surgical precision, David places it behind an oversized magnifying glass.

"Here's part of the problem." He points at a tiny burn mark with a pair of tweezers, "Oberheim stopped making these in '86. But I can get Sovtek replacement parts at Argon Electric."

The goateed man leans in.

"Sovtek? Sounds expensive," he grumbles.

"Not at all. Decommissioned Soviet missile technology. When the Berlin Wall came down in— is it two years ago already? Anyway, the—"

"I'm well aware of that. How much?"

"Well, the VCA's cooked, and she could use some TLC. So if you could shoot me, say $150, I'm picking up parts th—"

"Got change for $200?"

David hides his irritation at being interrupted a second time. He pulls a dilapidated wallet out of his pocket and opens it, revealing an unpaid parking ticket, a mess of receipts and a crumpled ten-dollar bill.

"Uh ..."

"Just tab the extra fifty. Can I get it tomorrow?"

"Tomorrow?!"

The bespectacled man pulls a wad of cash out of his pocket. David's eyes widen at the sight. He can finally cover the rent. He savors the crispness of the bills between his fingers as he takes payment, then leads the man toward the front of his house, past a pile of road-worn guitar cases and a small city of disassembled amplifiers. The man pauses and looks up at the spot where, yesterday, two bass guitars hung in a place of honor near the exit.

"At least they didn't take that one. She's my girl." David reaches up and caresses the strings of his beloved '63 Precision Bass. "I'll have your keyboard ready Monday. Tomorrow's super busy with New Year's plans. Come to think of it, it's my birthday on—"

The goateed man doesn't seem to give a hoot about David's birthday. He walks right past him and out the door, without looking back or acknowledging David's existence.

"*Dick*," David mutters.

He returns to his electronics lair-slash-living room. He picks up the cordless, presses a speed-dial button and is rewarded with a buzzing sound, a succession of musical beeps and a warbling ring tone. David switches to speakerphone as a female voice answers.

"Belinda Starkey here."

"Using your maiden name again?"

"What did you expect, David? Choices have consequences. And don't forget whose choice this was?"

"Yeah, yeah, still always right."

"I got your message. So what's this about your house getting broken into?

"I don't even want to talk about it. I must have scared them off when I got back from playing with Frankie.

"Frankie Sunshine? You're still playing with that ancient fossil?"

"Trying to make a living here."

"Did you report it to the police?"

"Pretty sure I know who did it."

"That answers that question."

"Anyway B, I just wanted you to know that I'm heading out now, to get the groceries for tomorrow."

Mid-conversation, David opens his kitchen window blind and looks out over the sunburned acre of scrubby wire grass that passes for a city park beside his house. He reaches for the birding binoculars he keeps by the window.

"God. You head-in-the-clouds musicians. It's today, not tomorrow, and I'm minutes away from your place," Belinda says, but David no longer hears her. His attention has been hijacked by what he sees across the park. He charges to a corner cupboard beside the fridge and slides out a tripod-mounted video camera. Then, with the phone tucked under his chin while trying not to trip over the mess of cords trailing him, he pushes the teetering set-up to the window.

"Sorry... bad reception!" he lies.

"I know you can hear me, David."

After toying with a tangle of wires on a patch bay, David powers up the camera and a grainy image flickers to life on a monitor above his workbench. He dims the blinds and zooms in on a group of street toughs gathered at a picnic table.

"Did you hear what I just said?!" Belinda barks.

As David fine-tunes the image into focus, the message being conveyed by the angry voice on the phone suddenly registers.

"Today? I thought you said—"

"David!" Belinda's voice shrieks through the speaker. "This is exactly what I'm talking about. Well I hope his room's ready, 'cause Zeke and I are parking *right now.*"

David presses End Call. He slams the phone on the kitchen counter, wondering why every conversation with Belinda has to end in a fight. He seems infinitely more concerned, though, with what's happening across the park. He watches as a hollow-cheeked man in a dark overcoat approaches the table. David snatches a VHS cassette off a nearby shelf and feeds it into the video machine's rectangular mouth. He presses Record and dims his workroom lights.

"That's it. Do something illegal and I'll get it all on tape. Just like last time," he mumbles. "Time to give me back my fucking bass!" David watches the monitor as an athletic man with blond hair and a militaristic buzz cut approaches the man. "Hmm. Haven't seen you before. Welcome to the neighborhood, *wanker.*"

Buzzcut glances over his shoulder then passes a leather satchel to the hollow-cheeked man. "Atta boy," David whispers in a gravely undertone. He checks his equipment. Everything is recording perfectly.

The gaunt-faced man tears the satchel out of buzz cut's hand. He looks inside it, then becomes furious. After a fierce verbal exchange, he hands over a cloth sack partially hidden within a plastic shopping bag. David has no way of hearing any audio, but the body language says it's tense.

He zooms in, presses a combination of buttons on his brand-new IBM Pentium 1 keypad, and a dot matrix printer starts grinding out a black-and-white image of the screenshot. David opens an envelope and removes a grainy picture of the same man, hand-labelled AADEN, a code name he's created for the suspicious looking individual, who he believes is a local criminal kingpin.

David is so focused that the metallic screech of his screen door grating open makes him wince. He turns and sees a four-year-old boy bounding full tilt down the hallway toward him.

"Daddy!" the boy shouts as he leaps into David's arms.

"Zeke! How are you, buddy? Daddy missed you."

Belinda enters the house, looking exhausted in charcoal-gray business attire, balancing a Star Wars knapsack in one hand

and a giant remote-control truck in the other. She nearly trips over a hodgepodge of shoes as she searches to find a place for Zeke's overnight supplies. She glances at the father-and-son reunion and a tentative smile creeps across her face. David looks over and spots her tender expression. He knows this won't go well.

"You know," he stammers, "I actually have to run an errand." He forces an optimistic tone into his voice. "But it will only take an hour ... or *two*."

Belinda's smile morphs into an irritated frown.

"This is the kind of BS I'm talking about, David. It's always something. Some lame excuse, some ridiculous—"

"If it makes you any happier, this is work-oriented," David replies through gritted teeth. "I have to get supplies for a client. You guys can hang here. I promise I won't be long."

Belinda rolls her eyes.

"Uh, no, thanks. The less time I spend in this dump, the better. Zeke, let's get lunch at Chuck E. Cheese."

"Yeah, Dad! Let's go."

"Sorry, buddy, Daddy's got some work to take care of. You go with Mom, and I'll see you back here soon. Okay, champ?"

"I guess so."

As Belinda whisks their son out of the house, David's not sure what's worse, Zeke's look of abandonment or Belinda's weary frown of disapproval. She lets the screen door slam behind her, just loudly enough to make sure he knows he screwed up. Again.

Chapter 5
Screen Siren

Since the end of the Cold War just two years ago in 1991, the shelves of David's favorite store, Argon Electric, have been overflowing with circuits previously available only behind the Iron Curtain. Ned McCarty, the store's proprietor, is an electronics genius, and David has heard persistent rumors that he's a former intelligence chief. Standing behind a long, glass-encased counter stuffed with box upon box of electronic paraphernalia, Ned reaches into a tiny drawer and retrieves a computer chip.

"This IC will work perfectly, David. It'll stabilize the notorious Oberheim tuning issues, and the bottom end of that beast will sound even bigger."

"Nice! Is this one of the better Soviet chips you've come across, Ned?"

"David, I've seen, handled, or reverse-engineered just about every circuit in the Soviet Space Program, but only once was I in the presence of their fabled SV-335 chip. Only three are known to exist. Well, two in a way, since one is stuck circling Mars as part of the Russian lander program. The others disappeared on the underground market last year. For ten million bucks."

"Oh come on."

"Even Project Blue Book is clamoring to get their hands on one, since they believe the circuit was harvested from a crashed UFO."

"As if," David scoffs.

"But, before I reveal any more state secrets, I'd better shut up," Ned replies with a smirk.

"Ned, Happy New Year, buddy. You've taught me everything I know about electronics. As usual, I could chat for hours, but the ex has me on the rails again."

"Great seeing you, David." Ned extends a hand, and David pulls him in with a one-armed hug. Ned recoils, mortified by such close human contact.

As David steps out of Argon Electric, he realizes that, as usual, he can't remember where he parked.

Not again.

He glances across the street and is struck by the sight of an elegant blonde woman walking toward a nearby transit stop. The woman seems strangely out of place in these pedestrian surroundings, wearing a blue chiffon dress, designer heels, hair teased under a gold-flecked scarf, and her eyes hidden behind Jackie O sunglasses. She has the grace of a Hollywood screen siren plucked from a Hitchcock film.

Mesmerized by the woman's allure, David watches as she seats herself at the end of the transit bench, where she takes a computer bag off her shoulder and places it at her feet. David admires her from afar, but with the weary realization that this picture of elegance is out of his snack bracket, he smiles to himself and shakes off a mild case of the what-ifs. He averts his attention and glances down the street, where a parking officer is ticketing his car.

"Hey!" David shouts.

He scoops up his supplies, but as he turns to leave he spots a gaunt man in a long overcoat hurrying toward the woman: Aaden.

David snatches a newspaper flyer from a nearby bench. He masks his face with it, then sits and lowers it beneath his eyes. He watches as Aaden walks up and stops unnaturally close to the woman. David's focus is suddenly derailed— by a loud and annoying street person that jumps out in front of him. The disheveled derelict, who wears multiple tattered coats and reeks of cheap wine, starts pestering for change.

"Alms for the hungry!" the vagrant cries. David tries to push him out of the way, but the man is deceptively strong and refuses to move. Only after David digs in his pants pocket, finds some coins and drops them in the stranger's tin cup does the vagrant shuffle off, mumbling and counting his take.

When David looks back across the street, Aaden is so close to the woman, his overcoat is nearly brushing against her back. And he's leering over her shoulder now, eyeing the computer case at her feet.

I better warn her, David thinks, but before he can take action, a city bus rounds the corner fifty feet away. With an engine roar it lurches toward the transit stop. As if prompted by the noisy vehicle, Aaden pulls a computer case out from under his coat. He places it on the ground, directly beside the woman's. David notices that the cases are identical in appearance, and are so close to each other, they are almost touching.

That's a bit weird, he thinks.

The bus arrives and blocks David's view, so he leans down, head almost touching the ground, and peers through a sooty cloud of diesel smoke. He can now see only hands and feet, but through the scurry of disembarking passengers, David watches as the woman reaches down and picks up the bag that Aaden has just set beside her. At the same time, the man's hand crosses hers and snatches the case that she has put down.

What the—

The passengers obscure David's view completely, and seconds later, when the bus leaves, the woman and man are nowhere to be seen, until he spots Aaden hurrying across the park, clutching the computer case which, a moment ago, was the woman's.

Curiosity piqued, David decides to follow him.

He ducks through alleyways and back streets, feeling his thirties catching up to him as he shadows the man from what he hopes is an inconspicuous distance. Aaden finally stops in front of a Gothic church building. He gazes warily in David's direction before opening a heavy wooden door just wide enough to slip inside the church's darkened entranceway.

David peeks out from a side alley as the door creaks to a close, then strolls nonchalantly past the building. He glances at a nameplate affixed to the archway wall:

Temple Of A Greater God.

The name is familiar to David. Maybe he heard it on the news, or perhaps he did a soul-destroying gig here that he'd rather forget. He glances up, trying to place the memory, then his eyes jolt open when he notices the time on the church's clock tower.

"Oh shit!"

Chapter 6
Sole Custody

When David Wesson arrives home in his exhaust-spewing Civic, he's relieved that Belinda's BMW is nowhere to be seen. He wheels into a parking spot and shuts the engine off. As he steps out of his car, David glances at the house and sees that its front door is wide open, the outer screen door swinging and banging in the blustery afternoon breeze. He retrieves his electronic supplies and approaches the house cautiously.

Knowing his ex-wife doesn't have a key and spooked by last night's break in, he makes a fist, leaving his large Honda key sticking out between his knuckles. David squeezes past the entrance and tiptoes down the hallway. He stops and peers around the living room corner, just as a human shadow darts past his workbench. David feels a surge of adrenalin. He steps in to confront the intruder.

"Jeezuz!" Belinda says. "You know I hate it when you sneak up on me."

At the far end of the room, Zeke is playing Super Mario Cart on Nintendo, oblivious to his dad's arrival.

"How the—" David glances at the young lad and lowers his voice. "—H.E. double-hockey-sticks did you get in here?"

Belinda dangles a door key on a silvery bass-clef chain.

"Under the mat? Seriously? And what is all this stuff?"

She points to the window camera and the documents scattered across the workbench. On the TV monitor, there's a jumpy freeze-frame image of Aaden.

"Two. Words," David snipes. "Privacy, please."

"Don't tell me you're back into that ridiculous hobby of yours."

"Hobby?!" David grunts as he covers the papers and shuts off the monitor. "At least I'm doing some good around here. This neighborhood is completely going to shi—."

He looks at Zeke and suppresses the urge to curse the neighborhood, his dwindling music career and the life choices that have brought him to this point.

"This is what I've been doing."

David holds up a newspaper and points to a tiny page-four article with the headline ANONYMOUS TIP LEADS TO DRUG ARRESTS.

"You are unbelievable," Belinda says.

She snatches the paper, scans the article, then flings it to the floor. She moves in close so Zeke can't hear.

"You do this when Zeke is here? How dare you put him at risk with this dangerous obsession of yours."

"Dangerous obsession? Give me a break. If you must know, I applied for a job with the Intelligence Service, so, just getting a little surveillance action here. God. I'd love to do a secret missi–"

"You? David Wesson ... a spy?" Belinda laughs dismissively. "Well at least there might be actual *paid* work in it, unlike this so-called music 'business' of yours. Careful what you wish for, though."

"What do you mean?" David asks, softening his angry tone.

"Remember what your uncle Jeffrey said from his deathbed. How he never got one good night's sleep after starting with The Agency, when he found out how insanely dangerous the world is."

"Uncle Jeffrey was suffering from dementia!"

"You seem awfully hyper, David. I can tell you've stopped taking your new medication. Why would you do that?"

"Those meds made me feel like I was going crazy. I flushed them."

"You need to give them more time! We don't need any more paranoid nervous breakdowns."

"Paranoid nervous breakdowns?! Perhaps a 'slight' exaggeration?"

"And what about the marijuana?"

"Not this again."

"You better be staying away from it. You're lucky your Dad paid attention to you for once in his life and brought in his lawyer."

"It was two joints! The whole thing was bullshit and that's why it got thrown out of court. I don't need to hear this for the fifty-thousandth time. Besides, it's 1993. Pot will be legal any day now."

"Dream on ... dream on," Belinda sings as she walks the short distance to the kitchen and opens the fridge door. "I see you haven't picked up any food."

She motions elegantly at its contents with an open hand, like a passive-aggressive Price Is Right model. David's antiquated Frigidaire is stuffed full—with twenty cans of Old Milwaukee, two stale pieces of pizza, a nearly empty bottle of pickled eggs and a withered ham-and-Swiss on a disintegrating bun.

"I was ... just about to do the shopping," David stammers.

"Ah, yes. The master procrastinator. Hard at play. Why do something today when you can do it the day after tomorrow. And did you ever file your taxes?"

The mere mention of the T-word opens a raw nerve.

"Don't start with that shit!"

Belinda stares Medusa-like at David, who feels himself turning to stone.

"What does shit mean, Dad?" a little voice asks from across the room.

"Zeke. We're leaving," Belinda announces.

Zeke shuts off his gaming console and comes running up to them.

"But what about the sleepover?"

"Come on, Belinda," David says, "Zeke and I can get the food together." He turns to Zeke. "Never too early for learning practical skills. Right, son?"

Zeke looks up at David, mystified by the comment, as mom collects his overnight bag. She takes their boy by the hand.

"You can come back tomorrow and stay with Dad for New Year's Eve."

"Great! Can I stay up until midnight?"

"Of course," David says as he follows them to the front door.

"Maybe Daddy will even clean up his house by then," Belinda jabs.

"It kinda looks like my toy room in here, dad."

Belinda collects their boy's sleepover gear, but as she leads him toward the door, she stops and faces David, suddenly more sad than angry.

"Can you at least start the new year by showing some responsibility? Maybe even a real job?" She turns and walks away with Zeke in tow. "Either that or 'two words': Sole. Custody."

Belinda leads their son down the crooked staircase toward the street. David slams the screen door behind them, but it bounces off its haphazard frame and springs open. As mother and son shuffle along his cracked concrete sidewalk, he hears Zeke singing a lullaby with his favorite new word.

"Shit shit shit. Shitty shit shit ..."

Chapter 7
Temple of A Greater God

Hours after Belinda and Zeke leave, David is still at his workbench, sipping on a warm beer. Beside him, three crumpled empties are lined up at tableside. He punches a code on his computer keypad and his workroom speaker lets out an angry buzz followed by the data screech of a dial-up modem. A moment later the sound mutes, a status message changes to Connected and a World Wide Web browser fades up on his Pentium 1's screen.

"Ned, you are a genius," David says.

He types Temple of a Greater God into a text box, hits Return, and a festive banner starts loading up, painfully slowly.

Happy New Year from Reverend Huracan. On the night of nights, only worship will save your soul.

Intrigued by this strange temple and curious about the computer case exchange he witnessed, David decides to investigate the matter further. He pounds back a final swig of Old Milwaukee, laces up a pair of Converse runners, and pulls on his favorite

Indian Motorcycle jacket. But as he collects his car keys and starts toward the front door, David glances at the lineup of empties on his bench. He sighs, then picks up the phone and dials Yellow Cab.

"Taxi to 1013 Northwest First Street. I'll be outside."

The red-orange winter sun is fading fast and David's flickering LED wristwatch reads 5:45 p.m. as he steps out the front door. By the time his taxi crosses into Overtown, a misty rain is falling and fog has rolled in from the Atlantic. David spots the twin spires of the church silhouetted against the murky sky and tells the driver to let him off a block away. He doesn't notice the '56 Studebaker that's been tailing them since Northwest and 3rd. The antique car pulls over a hundred yards behind them and it's headlights blink off. After paying a nine-dollar fare and begrudgingly leaving a one-dollar tip, David steps out into the dreary night.

In the darkness, the towering structure looks more like a haunted castle than a place of worship. David wonders for a moment why on earth he's doing this, but rationalizes that aside from the never-ending battles with his ex, his life is utterly devoid of drama. Between that and being fueled with liquid courage from his solo afternoon happy hour, David forges across the puddled sidewalk toward the church's decaying archway.

The Medieval-looking doors are locked up tight, so David walks to the side of the building and steps through an open chain-link gate. He's halfway across a slippery flagstone walkway that leads to the back, when a hearse lumbers into the parking lot, headlights glaring off the rain-soaked pavement.

David dives behind some thorny shrubs to avoid being spotlighted.

Maybe I should have stayed on those meds, he thinks. After the car passes, David sneaks his head up and watches as the boxy Cadillac slows and stops beside the double glass doors of the church's rear entrance. Two barrel-chested men in dark suits exit the funeral wagon and swagger, almost in sync, to the back of the vehicle. One of them opens the tailgate, and together, they roll an enormous casket out of the funeral wagon.

David jostles to dodge a stream of drips falling from a broken clay eave that happens to be right over his head. He looks up, cursing his rotten luck, and the church's Gothic architecture suddenly reminds him of Dunkeld Cathedral in his ancestral home of Scotland, which he visited with Belinda just before her surprise pregnancy. The cherished memory of a simpler time is interrupted by the rattle of the church's rear doors springing open. David crouches and watches as two indistinguishable figures emerge from inside. The taller of the two has heated words with the funeral men as they wheel the coffin inside and out of view.

After several tedious minutes of inactivity, his knees aching from squatting in the shrubs, David realizes he might as well turn around and make his way home. But after coming all this way and spending ten bucks of his hard-earned money on a taxi, he stands and creeps forward, but men suddenly reappear. David leaps back into the bushes, skewering his thumb on a thorn.

"*Owwch,*" he whispers.

Peering through the rain-soaked thorns, he sees that one of the broad-shouldered attendants is carrying a computer case that looks identical to the one he saw at the bus stop. At least this confirms he's witnessing something more than a chance encounter. It seems beyond circumstantial that this same case would show up with these lugs.

As the hearse wheels out of the lot, David spots a logo on its side door: Lucky Tiger Funeral Home. *What could possibly be lucky about a funeral home*, he wonders, as the vehicle bumps around the corner and vanishes into the mist.

Knowing he needs to get back to start cleaning house before Belinda shows up in a snit for the big sleepover tomorrow, David stands and brushes a scattering of leaves off his clothing. He turns to leave but thinks, *I've come all this way. What possible harm could come from spending another ten minutes here?*

David slips silently through the church's rear entranceway. After easing the door closed so it doesn't slam, he tiptoes down a musty parquet hallway, past bulletin boards and a darkened office. He encounters no one, which is fortunate since he hasn't yet devised a cover story should he be discovered. After what feels like an eternity sneaking around a lengthy creaky section, David finally arrives at the main chapel.

The vaulted ceilings of the church's inner sanctum are crisscrossed by a complex array of wooden beams, and a multitude of flickering candles illuminate the peaceful room. In sharp contrast to this serene setting, the coffin casts a forbidding shadow from atop a stage riser at the front. The thought of being in the same room as a cadaver makes the hairs on the back of David's neck bristle, but he continues forward into the softly lit refuge.

A side door suddenly springs open. A figure in a hooded robe appears, and David darts behind a row of prayer benches. His heart is pounding in his ears now, but he's been quiet and apparently hasn't been discovered. After taking a moment to settle, he peeks over the pew and sees that the robed figure is looking away from him, turning the pages of a scripture book.

Just as David begins to wonder what on earth he's doing in this ridiculous predicament, the silence is shattered by an ear-piercing *BEEP ... BEEP ... BEEP*. David looks down at the pager on his belt: Belinda calling. The man of the cloth spins and stares toward the source of the beeping. He rushes to the side of the stage, flips a switch, and the chapel's overhead lights blaze on like an electric supernova. Muttering the F-word under his breath, David fumbles with the clumsy pager, the one Belinda insists he must always carry. He finally shuts the annoying device off and considers making a run for it, but the momentary quiet is broken by the sound of slow and deliberate footsteps approaching.

David knows he's busted. He acquiesces and pulls himself to his feet, but when he looks up, he is stunned. Standing in front of him is the hollow-cheeked man, Aaden. Only now, he's wearing a reverend's collar.

"May I help you, my son?" Aaden says, his voice unexpectedly deep and soothing.

David searches for words, finding himself uncharacteristically tongue-tied.

"I'm ... here for the funeral," he stutters.

Aaden responds with a gentle smile.

"God be with you, child. The funeral is not until tomorrow. Might I offer a prayer in this time of—"

An explosive blast pummels the chapel. Its sound and shockwave are so jarring, David stumbles backward and off his feet. When he regains his composure and glances up, his ears ringing, the holy man looks like he's seen a ghost. The whites of his eyes showing, Aaden reaches down and tears the front of his robe open. Under his preacher's vestment, a vicious bloodstain is seeping through his crisp white shirt, expanding across his chest.

Aaden lets out a hollow moan. He staggers toward the front of the chapel, clutching at his heart as blood drips through his fingers, leaving a trail of crimson spatter behind him. The wounded man cries out and reaches for the casket to steady himself, but his clawing motion pulls on the massive wooden box. With a dreadful scraping sound, it starts rolling toward the front of the riser. David resists the primal urge to jump in front of the giant sarcophagus to prevent it from falling.

The coffin teeters across the edge as if in slow motion, then to David's horror, it tips over and crashes into the tile floor. A chunk of lid breaks off with a deafening crack and Aaden collapses to the floor beside it. David watches helplessly as the man convulses in death throes. Aaden opens his mouth as if attempting to say something, but after a long, gurgling exhale, his visage freezes into a final, gruesome mask, his lifeless eyes staring inanimately at David.

David feels his jaw quivering. His hands start to tremble. He looks down at Aaden, terrified of moving any closer and getting soaked in his warm blood. Then out of the casket, a trickle of white powder turns into a stream. A half-dozen shrink-wrapped packages tumble out of it onto the floor.

Finally, a cadaverous arm with a waxy-looking hand slides out of the cracked opening and smacks into the tiles with a meaty thud.

As David's eyes dart in a panic, he spots something in the darkened wings. At first he can't make out any identifying features, but it soon becomes undeniably clear that someone wearing a balaclava and leather gloves is moving silently through the shadows. The masked individual stops and slowly faces David. They stare at each other in silence for a moment, before the killer springs forth out of the darkness and charges him. As he approaches, David is taken aback by the attacker's crazed looking eyes. On the verge of full body contact, the assailant thrusts his hand forward.

"Catch!" he shouts.

David cowers and instinctively raises his hands to stop a heavy metallic object that is hurtling toward his face. The attacker runs right past him, then turns and vanishes down the back hallway, leaving David Wesson alone in the silent chapel— with two dead bodies and a blizzard of white particulate scattered across the floor.

An acrid cloud of gun smoke hangs in the air like The Reaper's deathly cloak as David looks down to see what he has caught. He drops a twelve-gauge shotgun at his feet.

Chapter 8
A Powdery Trail

David feels the floor move beneath him and realizes he's about to faint. Though he's always prided himself for being calm in a crisis, he's not used to the sight of blood, a stream of which is bubbling out of Aaden's chest and collecting in a sticky pool on the floor. David fights the urge to vomit.

This can't be happening.

He realizes that he needs to call the police immediately. He sees a phone near the front of the chapel and approaches it, but suddenly wonders, *How will I explain being here?* After extensive questioning, detectives would likely search his house, where he has pictures of the murdered man on his workbench. And when they interview Belinda, she'll recount that she saw Aaden's face on the TV monitor, and how David attacked her with a set of car keys. And even though David's "little misunderstanding" with marijuana, as his lawyer described it, was withdrawn almost a year ago, *the incident will show up on police computers,* he thinks. But most damning of all, David's fingerprints are now all over the murder weapon. He wishes he hadn't thrown out his medication, meant to dampen his obsessive ways. Had he been taking it as prescribed, he likely would have been at home playing Super Mario Cart in a Soma-like stupor– a preferable choice to becoming a murder suspect in a caper he never should have stuck his nose into in the first place.

David leaves a wide berth between himself and Aaden's crumpled body as he walks to the far side of the carnage, where the rectangular packages are scattered. Curious about the white substance, he dabs a finger in the powdery trail. David touches it to his tongue and the powder instantly produces a numbing effect that radiates through his mouth.

"Whoa!"

He flips one of the packages over with his toe and sees an embossed logo on its side: a falcon holding a dagger in its talons.

Cocaine, New Year's Eve, upcoming birthday, David thinks, but instantly shuts all illicit thoughts out of his head, since (a) addictive issues contributed to his marriage breakup, and (b) he needs to get away from here as quickly as possible, without bringing along anything that could tie him to this crime scene. His life is messy enough without being the primary suspect in a drug murder, where he'd be at the mercy of State Prosecutors in a city still reeling from a violent, decades-long Cocaine war. David decides to take his chances, cover his tracks and get the hell out of here.

He spots a closet at the side of the stage, so he picks the gun up and wipes it with a fallen piece of holy cloth. David cracks the 12-gauge open and sees a spent cartridge in the left barrel. After swabbing the gun one more time, he kicks it into the back of the closet under some stacking chairs. Terrified of leaving any telltale footprints, he wipes the floor behind him, then takes his shoes off and bangs them together, which produces a choking white cloud of coke. After dusting himself off, then cleaning the prayer benches and checking that he hasn't stupidly left anything behind like his new business cards, David bolts for the rear exit.

Chapter 9
Dangerous Dance

David slips through the church's rear doors. He wipes the handles with his shirt sleeve, but when he turns to leave, his blood ices. A police cruiser is parked on the street beyond the lot. Two officers in the car appear to be on a break or filling out a report, and the policewoman on the passenger side has her window open, so David moves silently. He crouches and puts his shoes on, then crawls toward the flagstone pathway on hands and knees.

"Possible shots fired at the Greater God Temple on Jefferson," a dispatcher's voice squawks over the car's radio.

"Copy that," the female officer replies. "320S. We are 10-7 at scene."

The police exit their vehicle with flashlights blazing. David is forced to scramble to the far side of the building, where he takes cover behind some garbage bins. Behind him is a wrought iron fence, and he concludes that jumping over it will be his only hope of getting away. But as he takes a deep breath in preparation, a flashlight beam glints off the metallic barrier in front of him.

David drops to the ground.

What to do, what to do?

He spots a discarded bottle and slithers to it on his belly. David picks it up, takes aim and lobs the bottle toward the flagstone pathway, where it lands with a clang and a crunchy rolling sound. The ruse works perfectly. The cops divert their attention to the flagstone area, and David capitalizes on their distraction. He takes an adrenalin-fueled vault over the fence and scurries off into the foggy night.

After ducking through a series of garbage-strewn alleys, David sees another police car patrolling the area, so he sticks to the shadows. Emerging onto a commercial street, he notices an English pub with a neon sign hanging above a Tudor-style entrance: The King's Cross. As David pauses in the alley to catch his breath, he finds himself trapped in a moral crisis. He realizes what he is doing is wrong. He needs to get back to the temple to speak with the police. But startled by the howl of a siren as a squad car rockets down the street fifty feet in front of him, David leaves that option behind. He quicksteps across the street and enters the small and lively pub.

He spots a table in a darkened corner near the back, so he walks in and seats himself. A tattooed server with a handlebar moustache approaches him almost immediately.

"What'll it be, chief?"

"Wild Turkey straight up, and a glass of ice water on the side."

"Important to stay hydrated," the server replies before returning to the bar.

As David tries to make sense of what has happened and what on earth to do next, a girl with waist-length black hair wobbles into the pub and stumbles up to the bar, incongruously tipsy for someone wearing a plunging leather catsuit and thigh-high boots.

"*Une verre de champagne, s'il vous plait,*" the girl slurs loudly in an exaggerated French accent. Several male patrons quickly take notice of her. One of them snuggles up to the leather-clad beauty and insists on putting her drink on his tab. She doesn't seem to dislike the attention.

The mustachioed waiter returns with the order and David knocks his bourbon back in one gulp. The Kentucky whiskey burns as it courses down his throat, but it's a reasonable tradeoff since his body starts to unwind. David closes his eyes to enjoy the dizzying flush, but when he opens them, the police duo he saw outside the church are standing inside the pub's front door. David raises his hand and scratches his forehead to hide his face, while he watches them through trembling fingers, wishing he'd ordered a double.

As he calculates the logistics of leaving through a back exit, if there is one, 'Another One Bites the Dust' starts blasting out of an old jukebox beside the barroom pool table. David watches as leather girl steps away from the beer-stained Wurlitzer, gyrating to the music. She swings her black mane around and struts to the beat, right up to him.

"Dance with me," she purrs.

David hesitates, but the feline one reaches for his hand. She pulls him out of his chair and starts swaying back and forth.

"I like you," she swoons, pressing her catsuited body into him.

"I... like you too."

David props the staggering girl up and dances with her, all the while keeping an anxious eye riveted on the cops. He notices the barman directing the officers' gaze toward the back corner where he sat a minute ago, so David leads the girl to the far end of the floor where the lights are low. The Emma Peel fashionista dances with crazed abandon, then stops and stares into his eyes.

"Would you think me too forward if I ask you to come to another place?" she says in broken English. "Avec moi? Ce soir?"

David has no idea how to respond, but all at once her fingernails dig into his hand like tiger claws. Leather girl looks him straight in the eye, suddenly stone-cold sober.

"We need to leave here. Now," she whispers, all traces of a French accent gone.

The girl glances at the police, then reprises her drunken barfly routine. David gets it. He follows her lead with an Oscar-worthy inebriated act. Then, keeping one eye on the cops while gaily soft-shoeing toward the exit, he swings the girl around and together, they sashay out the pub door.

Out on the street, the girl walks briskly. She leads David by the hand toward a pale-blue Mercedes sedan parked around the corner.

"What the hell's going on?"

"Get in. Your life depends on it."

Seeing no other option that could possibly end well, David climbs into the front passenger seat and shuts the door. Catsuit sits behind the wheel and fires up the car's powerful German engine. She kicks the pedal to the floor and the car rockets away from the curb.

"Who are you?" David exclaims, hurrying to buckle his seatbelt. He involuntarily presses himself back into his seat as she tears down the back streets while lighting a cigarette.

"Who am I?" she replies, laughing. "I'm the one asking the questions, Honeychile."

"God. Your driving is worse than my ex-wife's."

"You have no idea how badly you've screwed things up," the female Michael Schumacher replies as she downshifts and hairpins the wrong way down a one-way street. "Did Ennio contact you? Are you working for him?"

"Ennio?"

"You need to level with me. Now."

"Listen, lady, I'm a stay-at-home dad, a barely employed musician with one bee-otch of an ex-wife, and I have no idea what you're talking about."

"Why have you been tracking the package?"

"The package?"

The woman shakes her head, exhaling smoke. "I was afraid you'd say that. We'll have to do this the hard way."

David feels a tap on his shoulder. He turns and sees a silhouetted figure in the back seat. Before he can react, a heavy hand reaches out and grabs him by the collar. David looks down and watches the business end of a hypodermic needle plunge into his neck. The pain lasts barely a second before David Wesson's world goes dizzy and dark. He slumps forward in his seat, unconscious.

Chapter 10
No Escape

Groggy and confused, David opens his eyes and discovers he's in a cramped and dimly lit room, surrounded by khaki cases. A rumbling sound seems to emanate from the walls. He stretches his leg muscles, which are stiff and sore from chasing Aaden, but as he tries to stand, discovers that his wrists are bound to some cargo netting. He's so dizzy, it feels like the room is pitching up and down. David soon realizes that in fact, the room *is* being bumped around. *I'm in the back of a truck*, he thinks.

"Hey! Let me out of here!"

After a series of failed exclamations, then stomping vigorously on the floor, a narrow door swings open. An overhead light switches on, illuminating an impeccably dressed gray-haired man wearing a black waistcoat and white shirt, with a Windsor-cut collar and charcoal tie. The man hobbles up to David.

"Good day, sir. I trust you slept well."

"Where the hell am I?!"

"Oh dear. Let me remove those dreadful restraints. I hope I didn't put them on too tightly."

"You better bloody well take them off," David threatens.

"Oh I hope you're not going to act out," the elderly fellow says. "My Samoan friend, Mr. Pong, doesn't like it when guests misbehave."

David quickly puts the brakes on his bravado as a heavy-set man in a Hawaiian shirt appears at the doorway. The man's oversized arms look strong enough to bend pipe. The muscular Samoan stares down menacingly at David.

"Now, if you would please follow me. Oh! By the way, my name is Gilbert."

David rises to his feet and squeezes through the door, where he is forced to get up close and personal with the enormous Mr. Pong. Once clear of the hulking giant, raw instinct kicks in. David breaks to get away but sprints just a few feet into a narrow, tubular corridor before realizing that any hope of escape is futile. He's on an airplane.

Chapter 11
The Last Breakfast

The aircraft is an aging executive model with a gray interior and custom seating. Having grown up on military bases, David can tell by the cut of its wing that the plane is a 1940s-era DC-3. The polite man is unmoved by the enthusiastic getaway attempt and shuffles right past him.

"You must be starving," Gilbert says. "Allow me to fix you something. Would sausages and eggs suffice?"

An expressionless man seated at the front of the passenger cabin at a reverse-facing table looks up momentarily, then returns to playing a game of solitaire. He has the chiseled look of a soldier, with skull-and-dagger tattoos etched on sinewy forearms. The man points gruffly to a seat across the aisle and motions for David to sit.

"Actually, I really have to go to the bathroom."

"The door behind you on the left," Gilbert advises. "Usually Mr. Pong would escort you, but even if you did escape, well, I won't state the obvious."

David searches the bathroom in hopes of locating a makeshift weapon, but finds nothing deadlier than a box of cotton-tipped swabs. He pulls one out, rolls his eyes and tosses it over his shoulder for good luck. David exits the bathroom and is surprised to see that Gilbert has set a table for him near the front, complete with airplane-sized silverware and a French press filled with coffee.

"I'm terribly sorry for not introducing him sooner." Gilbert motions toward the tattooed man across the aisle. "This is Drago. And what might we call you?"

Drago looks drily at David.

"Let's just call me Mr. X," David replies, his inner rebel surfacing.

Drago glances at Mr. Pong, unamused.

"Well, do enjoy your repast, Mr. X.," Gilbert delights. "Oh heavens. I hope you're not a vegetarian."

Gilbert lifts the silver dome cover off a plate smothered in a breakfast of sausages, scrambled eggs, home-fried potatoes and baked beans. A glass of freshly squeezed orange juice sits on the side. David's eyes light up. He scarfs the food down like a condemned man.

"Mr. X?" Drago mutters in a thick eastern European accent.

"Correct," David says between chomps of a sausage he now holds in his hand. "If you look in the phone book under X, it's right there after Xaviera Hollander. God, this is good."

"Eat up, X. You don't have much time."

David's enthusiasm dwindles.

"Not so hungry anymore. But that coffee ..."

He reaches for the French press, but Mr. Pong wraps his fingers around David's forearm with a titanium grip.

"The coffee will have to wait," Drago says. "Who you are working for?"

"Work? If only. Nothing at the moment, but I'm auditioning for the Singing to the World Showband tomorrow." His brow furls. "Unless today is tomorrow."

"Why you are tracking the package?" Drago presses, in what David recognizes as a Slovenian accent.

"The package? Why do people keep asking me that?" David says, although he finally realizes that this entire misadventure has everything to do with the computer bag exchange he witnessed. But he reveals nothing and looks longingly at the coffee.

"Just one sip?"

He pushes his hand toward it, but Pong tightens his bone-crushing grip.

"Cripes! Take it easy."

Drago sighs, weary of David's flippant attitude.

"You work for Ennio?"

"Who the hell is Ennio? Sounds familiar, but none of this makes any sense at all."

Drago exchanges a tired look with Pong, then picks up a phone mounted on a fuselage bulkhead. He speaks into it, but David can't hear what he's saying above the engine noise.

"Roger that," Drago says.

He hangs up the phone, then stands and walks to the front of the cabin, where he grabs a metal handhold. The aircraft suddenly noses into a steep descent.

Mr. Pong forces David out of his seat. He starts shoving him toward the rear of the plane.

"Are we landing?" David asks.

"That is one way of looking at it," Drago replies in his broken English.

The plane levels off as a male voice crackles over the speaker.

"Altitude 1500, speed 110 knots. Waypoint Zebra, I repeat: Waypoint Zebra."

"Sadly, Mr. X, there won't be time for that coffee," Drago announces.

Pong releases a latch and slides the exterior door of the plane open. The roar of hurricane-force air is deafening.

"Who are you?!" Drago shouts, seething with anger now.

Mr. Pong pushes David into the open doorway and forces him to look down at a jungle canopy rushing past.

"I'm nobody. I swear!"

"One more time," Drago presses. "Who do you work for?!"

"Look, I'm a B-list bass player who can barely get a wedding gig. Please. Don't do this. I've got a kid."

"I couldn't care less about kid," Drago shouts. "Mr. Pong. You tire of these infantile games?" Pong responds with a sour-faced grunt. "Then throw Mr. X from the plane."

"Oh jeezuz, no," David pleads. "I don't know anyone named Ennio."

Pong forces David's head out the door. The tornadic blast of air feels like it's going to tear the skin off his face. Mr. Pong starts squeezing his massive body against David's back. David feels himself being pushed forward, reaching the point of no return.

"Hold up!" a strong female voice commands.

Pong pulls David in and latches the door closed behind him. David crumples to the floor, broken.

"Congratulations, Mr. X. Correct answer," the female voice says, in a soft but confident tone. I hope you understand that we needed to be sure."

David looks up. Standing in front of him is the blonde woman from the bus stop, except now she is dressed in a cool, crisp pilot's uniform.

Chapter 12
Angry Vortex

David Wesson stares up at the statuesque pilot, whose blonde hair is slicked into a ponytail under her captain's hat. He attempts to stand, but events of the last twenty-four hours have taken their toll. Pong lifts him to his feet.

"You? A woman of considerable talents."

"And then some," she replies with a knowing look.

Drago rolls his eyes. He returns to his seat, but Pong remains steadfast by the woman's side.

"Why am I here, what do you want with me? And who are you?"

"So many questions, Mr. X. Or should I say, David Wesson?"

"How the—"

"All in good time, David. But right now my considerable talents, as you say, are required to land this old bucket."

The plane suddenly hits a pocket of turbulent air.

"Can you at least tell me your name?"

"To these men, I'm Captain Bisset. But after all I've put you through, I'll allow you to call me Sophie."

The name has just the right amount of exotic, David thinks.

Sophie switches into all-business mode and makes her way to the cockpit. The plane rocks and shudders, and soon a flash of light is followed by a grumble of thunder.

"Buckle up, boys, a bit of weather ahead," she announces as she enters the cockpit and shuts the door behind her. The aircraft pitches as David returns to his seat, where Gilbert has stowed the dining table.

"Do put your seatbelt on, sir," he advises. "Severe thunderstorms are quite common around the island."

"Ah yes. 'The island'," David says sarcastically.

Gilbert seats himself in a reverse-facing service position and tightens a four-point harness across his chest. As David buckles up, he glances across the aisle at Drago then does a wide-eyed double take, shocked to see that the mercenary is suddenly a quivering shadow of his former self.

"I hate this place," Drago whimpers, looking more like a sad-faced clown than a soldier of fortune. He grips a set of rosary beads and kisses a cross that hangs around his neck on a gold chain. The Slovenian pulls a flask out of his pocket.

"What pla—" David is silenced by a blinding flash and a stomach-churning jolt of turbulence. The plane heaves as another burst of lightning and a nearly simultaneous thunderclap follow. Even Mr. Pong scrambles into a seat and belts himself in. Drago takes short, rapid breaths now, like a woman giving birth.

"Hoo... hoo... hoo..."

"My apologies, Mr. X. I for one prefer landing under more ... tepid conditions," Gilbert says, but David is onto another critical issue.

"Hey, uh, mind if I?"

He motions at Drago, hand to mouth, the international sign for 'Can I have a drink?' Drago passes the flask toward him as a wind gust hammers the plane. Drago's flask is torn from his hand. It bounces off the plane's ceiling, but David flips his hand out and snatches it midair.

"Thank you," he mouths to Drago, then unscrews the lid and knocks back a belt of what must be double-proof Russian rocket fuel. David's face curdles.

"Special brew from hometown," Drago says.

Gilbert is pushed to his limit of politeness, but he dutifully reassures David.

"I'm afraid it's often like this near Skeleton Bay. Damned weather experiments. I don't like them one bit."

The sky is now a dark, angry vortex. The engines roar as hail starts pelting the fuselage, sounding like a thousand nail guns firing at its thin aluminum skin. The wings of the old beast flex and groan, pummeled by furious gusts. Just as Drago shuts his eyes and starts mumbling a prayer, lightning hits the plane with a blinding flash and a simultaneous ka-BANG.

Multiple alarms start beeping from behind the cockpit door. "Sink rate ... Sink rate," a programmed voice starts repeating. David looks out his window and sees the tops of trees whizzing past, yards away. Captain Bisset's voice crackles through a speaker that now hangs unattached from the ceiling on its electrical wires.

"Brace yourself for landing. Brace yourself for— Crash positions!"

Drago screams like a terrified infant as the DC-3's landing gear slams down hard on a jungle runway. An enormous spray envelops the plane, but in an instant, things go strangely quiet.

"That wasn't so bad," David says, almost in jest, but Drago, hysterically begs to differ.

"No. That bad. That ve-ry bad."

Gilbert clarifies.

"The plane has merely bounced, sir. In just a moment we'll be— Aaaaaahh!"

David also screams as the aircraft pounds back onto the tarmac, which looks more like a riverbed than a runway. The Pratt & Whitney engines sound as if they're going to explode as the props lever into reverse-thrust. Still travelling at eighty knots or so, the aircraft begins to yaw sickeningly to one side.

"Nothing to get all a-twitter about," Gilbert lies, his voice cracking.

Now they're going sideways, almost backwards, while being buffeted by radical G-forces. David looks out the window and sees that the plane is hurtling toward a huge, monolithic ground sign. A collision seems unavoidable. But with a solitary squeak of rubber and a gentle bounce, the plane glides to a stop, barely ten feet shy of the massive sign, which reads:

Welcome to Andros, Bahamas. Have a sunny day!

The engines power off and the propellers spin down, creating a welcome silence. Captain Sophie Bisset emerges from the cockpit, looking as cool as a nighttime summer breeze. She gazes out at the four men cowering in front of her.

"That's the most fun I've had in weeks."

ACT TWO

Chapter 13
Listen Up

Captain Bisset is remarkably unfazed by the near-disastrous landing. Behind her, through an open cockpit door, a co-pilot works up post-flight procedures while Gilbert begins to tidy the cabin.

"Listen up," Sophie announces. "Drago and Pong. Everything into the van."

"The sooner I'm out of this deathtrap, the better," Drago mumbles.

"Somebody better tell me what the hell is going on around here," David blurts.

"Hang tight, David," Sophie says. "Once we're through customs, I'll explain everything and bring you up to speed."

"Customs?! You people have no idea how much shit I'm in if I'm not home tonight."

"Always try and see the glass half-full, sir," Gilbert advises, "Now, here is your passport. Do endeavor not to misplace it."

"David *Smith?*"

"We thought it best not to use your family name, so your middle name will have to suffice."

"David Smith Wesson?" Drago scoffs from the back of the plane. "As in the Smith and Wesson gun?"

"Brilliant, Drago! And no one's ever joked about my name before," says David sarcastically. "What can I say? I had cruel parents."

Sophie pulls David in close.

"Your story is simple. You are David Smith. You're playing with the band tonight at the Breakwater Mansion. Everything else stays the same—your birthday, address, everything. Got it?"

"Who's this band I'm playing with?"

"The Nova Sound Explosion," Gilbert replies. "Oh, they're wonderful. Last year in Boca, they performed a delightful version of"—Gilbert twists and sings— *"Tie a yellow ribbon, da dee doo dee daaa."*

"So you drugged me, kidnapped me, and flew me here to play bass with a bunch of lounge lizards?"

"Everything will soon be crystal clear, David," Captain Bisset assures him, "but for now, it is of utmost importance that you stick to the story."

"Yeah, yeah. I'm David Smith, playing with the Nova Sound Explosion at the Breakwater Mansion, and I'm from—"

A low-pitched vibration signals that the plane's exterior door is being opened. A delicious wave of tropical air floods the cabin. A young customs official dressed in khakis steps aboard. She's followed by a wide-shouldered Bahamian man wearing gray slacks, with a laminated security badge clipped to the front of his polo shirt. A smile breaks across his face when he sees Captain Bisset.

"What da vybe is," he says, the local expression rolling off his tongue in a soothing Caribbean baritone.

Sophie's eyes light up. "Tony!"

"My god, girl! Look at you," the man with the security badge replies. "That's some weather you landed in. I obviously taught you well."

Another voice of recognition follows. "Hello, Tony."

"Gilbert! It's been too long. You look well, my good man."

"A little worse for wear after that landing, but otherwise, still this side of the grass," Gilbert says. Tony rushes over and embraces Gilbert with a giant bear hug that lingers.

"Now, now. Try not to crush me, and don't get all huggy like the kids these days, but yes, it is wonderful to see you, Tony."

"Lady and Gentlemen," Tony announces, "if you would kindly present your passports to Shirell here, we shall soon be under way."

Shirell seems anything but kindly as she approaches David and takes his travel document.

"Where were you born?"

"Washington, DC."

"Occupation?"

"Musician."

"Quaint. What are you doing in the Bahamas?"

"Playing tonight at the Breakwater Mansion."

"With the Nova band?"

"Yes, ma'am."

"What's your middle name?"

Sophie glances over below the radar, but David handles himself with expertise. Being a musician, he's used to being grilled and marginalized at border crossings.

"No middle name," he replies.

Shirell looks down at his passport, then back up at him. "That's a bit unusual."

"I come from an unusual family," David explains, completely telling the truth.

She watches him for telltale signs of nervousness, but after a lengthy poker-faced stare, Shirell scribbles her signature and stamps his passport.

"I hope you'll be playing Brown-Eyed Girl at the party tonight."

"Just for you," David says, hiding his disdain for the song, acquired after playing a billion bad versions of it on jams and jobbing gigs.

The customs officer moves past him and takes Sophie's documents.

"Grab your things, everyone," Tony says. "Sophie, your car is out front. You and David follow me. The others will meet us at Skeleton Bay."

"Very good, Tony," Sophie replies as Shirell stamps her passport.

David tags along as they deplane down a scuff-marked set of aluminum stairs and walk toward a bright yellow, two-room airport building. The morning is a humid seventy-five degrees and the storm already a distant line of clouds a mile to the south. Pong effortlessly tosses a suitcase at David, who nearly wrenches his back when he catches it. Tony directs them toward a gate reserved for private planes, and Gilbert follows last in the group, sweating and struggling with an oversized bag. Barely ten feet from the exit, a humorless immigration official steps out of a hidden door.

"Hold up!" the man says. "Which one of you is David Smith?" David raises a finger. "Got a work permit?"

Unspoken tension floods the group, and for the first time David feels tongue-tied, never a good thing at customs. He checks his pockets to buy some time as Captain Bisset walks over to assess the situation. Just then Gilbert arrives, out of breath from pulling the giant suitcase.

"Oh, drat. So sorry," he says. He pulls a document out of his waistcoat and passes it to the customs man. "I believe this is what you're looking for."

After checking the document over, the official hands it to David.

"Indeed it is. Keep this with you at all times while you're here. Understood?"

"Yes, sir."

The group begins making their way toward the gate, when the official raises a hand again.

"One more thing! Tony, for God's sake, man. Can you help the gentleman with his suitcase?"

A look of alarm passes over Tony's face. He rushes over and takes the enormous bag from Gilbert, who looks ready to drop. Gilbert thanks the customs man with a respectful bow.

"Bless you, sir."

As they exit the tiny airport, a salty ocean breeze welcomes David Wesson, now David Smith, to a tropical vista of pink and purple bougainvillea, grizzled mangrove trees and towering coconut palms.

Chapter 14

Clever Boy

Gilbert follows Tony toward a beaten up Chevy Impala parked beside the terminal, while David hurries to catch up with Sophie as she walks toward a ragtop Land Rover.

"Finally ready to share the joy? It's hard to believe you people abducted me for my bass-playing prowess."

Sophie removes her pilot's cap and shakes out her blonde hair.

"All good with the Rover, Tony?"

"Affirmative. We swept her and she's clean."

"Roger that. You guys go ahead. David and I are going to take the scenic route."

Tony flashes her a thumbs-up, then he and Gilbert climb in the Impala and rumble off.

David clambers into the Rover, but is startled to discover that he's sitting in the driver's seat.

"Whoa. Wrong side of the road."

"Wanna drive?"

"Maybe not."

He scrambles to the left passenger side as Sophie jumps in and fires up the vintage four-by-four's custom engine. Bajan dance music erupts from a hot-rodded sound system, jolting David's already frayed nerves. Sophie turns the volume down to a less bone-rattling level as she wheels out of the airport onto a freshly paved road surrounded by swamps and tropical vegetation.

"You have a lot of questions, David, and I'm going to make this as simple as possible."

David listens intently – rare for him. "But first," Sophie says. She tosses him a tiny object. David catches it, then slowly opens his fingers.

"A wedding ring?"

"An engagement ring."

Sophie flashes a matching diamond band on her fourth finger.

"You and I are to be married."

David looks down at the ring then up at Sophie as she hangs right onto a gravel trail. The Land Rover's throaty engine revs to the limit as it drifts around the corner.

"Go ahead. Size nine, yes?"

"No way. This is too bloody weird. Besides, no more marriage for this kid."

"Just do it. By the way, you might want to put your seatbelt on."

David snaps his belt in as Sophie veers onto a dirt trail. But instead of slowing for the rugged conditions, she downshifts and hits the gas.

Sophie checks her pockets. "You don't have any cigarettes, do you?" she says.

The odd timing of Sophie's question triggers an equally odd memory for David.

"That was you! Holy shi— Watch out for that ... Never mind."

The four-by-four hits a rut as it rounds a rain-soaked corner, spewing a fountain of mud and narrowly missing a gnarled old Caribbean pine.

"You're the black-haired girl from the bar. The one all hot for me with that *voulez-vous coucher avec moi* routine."

"Clever boy. Hang on!"

Sophie tightens her grip on the wheel, kicks her foot to the floor, and the Land Rover becomes airborne over a pebbled creek bed. It slams back into the ground and careens toward the edge of a fast-approaching cliff, beyond which lies a white-capped bay.

"You do see that the road ends ahead, yes?" David shouts.

"Huh?"

Sophie takes her foot off the gas, pops the handbrake, and the vehicle does a forty-five-degree slide on a patch of sandy soil. It stops barely six feet shy of land's end. David is frozen in his seat with his mouth hanging open as she kills the engine and jumps out.

"Come on!" she shouts.

Sophie runs full tilt toward the edge of the cliff. After a glance over her shoulder to egg David on, she leaps off, her legs kicking the air as gravity pulls her downward and out of sight. David extricates himself from the Land Rover, whose engine is crackling, pinging, and smelling of burnt oil now. He creeps toward the brink, some fifty feet above ocean waves crashing on rocks below. Not a huge fan of heights, David feels his heartbeat quickening as he secures his footing. He grabs a scrubby pine and leans out over the edge.

"Boo!"

Five feet below him, Sophie is seated cross-legged on a grassy outcropping, surrounded by flowers and a tangle of tropical plants. She smiles and lets her head fall back. David climbs down, cautiously at first, then, *Oh, what the hell.* He releases the withered tree and tumbles into the mossy grass beside her. They lay there together in silence for a moment, gazing at the azure sky as cotton-ball clouds tumble past, blown by the morning trade wind. Soaking up this rare tranquil moment, David feels oddly at peace. He rolls his head to the side and faces her.

"Is this the part where Rod Serling appears in a black suit?" he says.

Sophie squints in puzzlement.

"Oh puh-lease don't tell me you've never seen the original Twilight Zone series."

"I'm not nearly old enough to have seen that," Sophie digs, suppressing a wry smile.

"Ouch!" David grimaces.

Undaunted, he grits his teeth and launches into a near-perfect Rod Serling impression.

"They say a dream takes barely a second, yet in that space of time, one can live an entire life. And which is the reality? The one we know, or the one in... the Twilight Zone. Or something like that," he says.

Sophie seems to be caught off guard by the intimacy of the moment. She stares deeply at David, who rolls off his back and props himself up just above her on his elbows, intimately close, face to face.

"Okay, Mrs. Wesson. You've got a lot of explaining to do."

Chapter 15
The Precipice

Sophie is unimpressed by David's affected machismo. She rolls away from him and sits up.

"Okay. Here goes. About eight months ago, you applied for a job."

"A job?" David's eyes scan back and forth, then his expression brightens. "You mean... with the Intelligence Service?"

Sophie responds with a nod and a raised eyebrow.

"So you're saying that I—" David says.

"Congratulations. You got the job."

"No way."

"Yes way."

"O-kay," David replies suspiciously.

The reason you're here, is that you're now part of an operation. One of utmost importance."

"But how? Nobody contacted me."

"Someone gave us a recommendation, and we've been vetting you for almost two years."

David is both astonished and mystified. "Who recommended me?"

"That's not information I usually divulge, David, but in light of all I've put you through, I'll make an exception. It was Ned McCarty."

"Ned? From Argon Electric? So he is a senior intelligence operative."

"Officially, I can neither confirm nor deny that."

"Or you'd have to kill me?"

"Well, not me personally," Sophie replies drily, dampening David's enthusiasm.

"Ned's an electronic genius. He taught me everything I know."

"Yes, we're aware of that. But just so you hear it from me, I voted against you being on my team," Sophie says.

David barely hears her, shocked at how his life has gone from the mundane to the sublime literally overnight. He's never been a creature of habit or routine, but he *is* an expert at flowing with change. His chosen field of music has been one of towering highs and crushing lows, so David has an uncanny ability to adapt, and quickly. His father was a hard-boiled military officer and one tough hard-ass of a father. Growing up in his strict, authoritarian regime, David learned the concept of discipline, but he also engendered a wild, rebellious side.

"You're a loose cannon, David. In this business, one misstep, even one wrong expression, can get you – and others – killed."

"How are you connected to all of this?"

"My father is a legendary agent," Sophie replies, "but only a few people way up the flagpole are privy to that knowledge. I grew up in a world of special ops and was officially recruited at age eighteen."

"The danger and worry sent my uncle Jeffrey to an early grave," David says, a tinge of sadness in his voice.

"Jeffrey Savard. My father worked with him on many occasions. Dad was real torn up when he passed."

"You people have done your homework. How do you cope?"

"I learned to live for the present."

"Yeah, I noticed that. But why am I here?"

"A number of reasons. Your superb electronic abilities, your adaptability, your *acceptable* fitness level and intellect, your military upbringing. Plus, since you are a man of music, we can get you close to a person of interest tonight at a New Year's function."

"'Person of interest'?"

"Your hobby of filming the local drug dealers compromised our mission, brought unwanted attention and prompted a diabolical event to happen tonight."

"Oops."

"On top of that, we had an agent go rogue last year, which allowed enemy milestones to be reached months, maybe even years ahead of schedule. This operative was playing both sides, and doing it well."

"Who is this double agent?"

"We don't know. But he goes by the name, 'Ennio'. Ring any bells?"

"Ah yes. The guy you were going to throw me out of a plane over."

"I did apologize," Sophie reminds David. "I can only reveal partial details to you at this time. You're obviously aware of the Temple of a Greater God."

David cringes.

"On second thought, don't answer that," Sophie says. "The temple is run by a charismatic leader who goes by the name of Reverend Huracan. He's convinced his followers that he's a living god, and they will do anything for him. But he's also a weapons smuggler and drug dealer, heavily funded by a number of foreign entities, including: North Korea, the Russian mob, and the Colombian cartel."

"Heavily funded to do what?" David asks.

"To launch a major terror event over the next twenty four hours. That's his estate over there."

Sophie points to a palm treed compound across the white-capped bay that features a colonial mansion, a lengthy concrete dock, and a scattering of cottages. A quarter mile offshore, a huge motor yacht is at anchor. She hands David a gyro-stabilized monocular.

"Quite the boat. Is that a helipad at the front?"

"Yes, it is," Sophie replies. "That's Reverend Huracan's yacht, the Lucky Tiger. She's worth about thirty million."

"Sweet ride."

"And that's for what you see above the water. Intel suggests he has a private submarine underneath it. But, enough for now. We've got to check in at Skeleton Bay, get you a change of clothes, and fit you for scuba gear."

"Scuba? I'm perfectly happy on dry land."

Sophie holds her hand out and helps him up the precipice. "You'll be fine."

As they walk toward the Land Rover, David looks more like a frightened little boy than a secret agent, shuffling and staring at his feet.

"Oh come on," Sophie says, in almost a mothering tone.

"Yeah, yeah. But there's one thing that would really help to ease my stress level." Sophie looks back at him with a sideways glance. "Can I drive?"

Chapter 16
Ruthie

The ride out is excruciating for Captain Bisset. She never lets anyone drive her baby, but knowing what lies ahead for David and what will be expected of him over the next twenty-four hours, she gives him a rare pass. David is no slouch behind the wheel, and he pushes the modified safari vehicle beyond even Sophie's comfort level. After howling at him to slow down on every corner, then being a terrified passenger while he drives on the left side of the road for the first time since his Scotland adventure five years ago, Sophie is exhausted by the time they reach the turnoff for Skeleton Bay.

She directs him down a dirt laneway and they soon arrive at a rustic lodge on a point of land with the ocean a mere hundred feet away. David is struck by the beauty of the setting. Aquamarine waters sparkle with diamond clarity, and a mile offshore, waves break over a coral reef that stretches as far as the eye can see. He parks beside a rugged stone and wood-timbered building, then Sophie leads him to an outdoor patio where

Tony and Gilbert are sipping drinks at a tiki hut bar. Gilbert looks much less formal sans waistcoat and tie, tipping a cocktail as his white shirt luffs in an onshore breeze.

"Might I get another Goombay Smash?" he asks a young bartender. "Although that first one is going straight to my head."

The well-tanned lad nods and gets to fixing another tumbler of the local rum specialty.

"I'm amazed she let you drive," Gilbert says. "She never lets anyone near Ruthie."

"Ruthie?" David turns to Sophie with a half-cocked smile on his face. "That's what you call your car?"

"Yeah. She's my girl," Sophie replies lovingly. "But more importantly, I hope you were listening to my briefing notes."

"What you were saying in between all that yelling? I was. And you're a terrible back-seat driver, by the way."

Sophie shrugs.

Tony, Skeleton Bay's proprietor, is constantly on a cordless phone coordinating the logistics of the lodge's business. He covers the mic and faces Sophie.

"You guys should check in. Cabin seventeen," he says. "Your bags are there."

"Not to worry, young man," Gilbert reassures David. "I put some clothing together for you and you will look absolutely smashing. Speaking of smashed, I'm now going to wobble off to my quarters for an afternoon nap."

"The Rev will be here at twelve thirty, a half-hour from now," Tony says, a hint of concern on his brow as he hangs up the phone. "He's never late, so this would be a good time to make yourselves scarce. There's food there, so eat up. It's going to be a busy afternoon."

"Good plan, Tony. It's cleaner that way," Sophie says, "C'mon, David."

David is overflowing with questions, but at this point realizes it's better to just stay out of the way. Sophie leads him down a forested pathway toward a rustic cabin nestled among a cluster of coconut palms. Inside the bright and cheery suite, batik curtains sway to the ocean breeze through open shutters, and waves can be heard lapping at the nearby sandy shore.

"Is this where we'll be spending our wedding night, honey?" David says, feeling unexpectedly prudish as he stands in front of the room's queen-sized bed, trying to cover his shyness with bravado.

"In your dreams!" Sophie says while she opens her suitcase at the end of a short hallway.

A look of terror suddenly passes over David's face.

"Oh no!"

Sophie rushes up to him.

"What's wrong?"

"My ex is bringing Zeke for a New Year's sleepover tonight. I have to call her."

"Not a chance," Sophie says. "No calls."

"What?! You cannot be serious."

"David, I can't imagine what that creative brain of yours is going through right now, but calling home is completely out of the question. Besides, she is your ex, right?"

"Oh nice. Our first fight. And we haven't even had our first dance."

"Listen. I can put you on the next flight out of here. If you decide to leave, I will understand, but everything will soon be revealed. You'll be fully briefed this afternoon, then read into the mission."

"What have I gotten myself into?" David laments.

"I'm still not at liberty to say, but one thing is certain: If you opt out now, you won't be asked to join an Intelligence Agency again. Ever."

David closes his eyes and rubs his forehead.

"So, what's it gonna be?" Sophie says.

"Can someone at least get a message to Belinda and Zeke?"

"No."

"I just don't want to lose my kid to this sole custody thing she keeps throwing in my face."

"Look. Even if you did return to Miami, which you can, you wouldn't be allowed to contact anyone. You'd be quarantined in a safe house for at least a week."

David realizes that he's trapped, a victim of his own curiosity.

"So this is what Belinda meant when she said, 'Careful what you wish for'. Dammit! I hate when she's right."

David ambles over to the window and gazes out at the sea. He weighs his options, then sighs heavily.

"All right. I'm in."

"You're sure."

David straightens his posture as if at attention.

"Absolutely. One. Hundred. Percent."

"Good. Then I'm going to put my feet up for an hour. You... are stressing me out!"

Chapter 17
Danger Boy

David feels awkward being in such close quarters, having met Sophie only hours ago under surreal circumstances. Sophie, however, trained for unusual and stressful situations while leveraging human assets, seems perfectly at ease as she immerses herself in a shower while David opens his suitcase. He discovers that Gilbert has curated an excellent wardrobe for him. *The old guy's got taste*, David thinks, as he changes into khaki skateboard pants, a blue tee and red Nikes. Sophie slips into a midnight-blue one-piece bathing suit that she wears under tan capris and an ivory linen tank top. She steps out of the shower room, its steam surrounding her like a full body halo.

"You are in some good shape, girl."

"Well, been slacking a little. I can do twenty chin-ups on a good day. Right now, though, I need rest."

"I understand. Must be exhausting, what with all the kidnappings, crash landings, interrogatio—"

"And that was the easy part," Sophie assures him. "Buck up, Danger Boy."

"Danger Boy? Oh god. What have I done to deserve this?"

David leaps onto the bed and strikes a superhero pose, pulling his shorts up into his crotch, like tights. After zero sleep and too much stress, Sophie suppresses a smirk. David senses her approval.

"This is a job … for Danger Boy!" he announces in a deep, manly voice. He puffs his chest out like a peacock while making sputtering trumpet sounds with his lips. Next, he bounces into the air with a Bruce Lee–inspired flying kick that morphs into a heroic sword-fighting move. He comes dangerously close to slicing the top of his head off on a whirring ceiling fan.

"Look out!" Sophie shouts.

He eventually dies a drawn-out, melodramatic death on the bed, then sneaks one eye open to see her reaction. Sophie just shakes her head. She lies back and takes some calming breaths, but her Zen-filled aspirations are punctuated by giggles. Her impish smile gradually fades, though, and she drifts into an exhausted slumber.

David is anything but tired after his superhero pageantry. He paces the room, then snatches a conch roll and a piece of Johnny Cake from Tony's food platter. He wanders outside, where he discovers a raised sunning platform by the sea. David climbs up onto the six-foot-high perch and reclines into a chaise longue that overlooks a calm and sheltered bay. Though grateful for a moment of serenity, the realization that he will be unable to contact Belinda and Zeke gnaws at him. The breakup with the mother of his son has been soul-crushing, but he still cares for her deeply. The love he feels for Zeke is unparalleled by anything he's ever experienced, but marriage and fatherhood have not been easy for David, after years of being rudderless and free.

He's distracted from his worries by the sound of tires on gravel. David looks down and watches as a white van slows and stops, then backs up to the water's edge beside him. Drago jumps out of the driver's door wearing a fleece hoodie over a wetsuit and hurries to the rear of the van, where he is joined by his passenger, Mr. Pong. The burly Samoan unlatches the back doors and retrieves a pair of khaki cases, the ones David saw on the plane. He passes them to Drago, who ferries the cases through the shallows and loads them onto a pontoon boat. Next they load up diving equipment, placing air tanks aboard the boat in partitioned compartments.

The sound of a driving Caribbean bass line catches David's ear. It sounds like it's blasting out of bass-heavy speakers upshore. He decides to investigate the music's source and climbs down from the platform, but when he returns to the cabin to check in with Sophie, he finds her rolled onto her side, sound asleep. David stands in the doorway and smiles. He fantasizes how, if this were another time and setting, he might lie down beside this fascinating creature and nuzzle lovingly into the back of her neck and soft blonde hair. David's better instinct tells him that this scenario best remain a fantasy. Aside from the fact that they barely know each other, the captain likely has commando training, and with a single scissor-kick-reversal could pin him into submission between her well-toned thighs. The notion of being subdued on the bed by Captain Sophie isn't the worst thought that's crossed David's mind today either, but he decides instead to wander up the beach on his own.

As David approaches the thatched-roof bar, he looks out to sea and notices that the Reverend's super-yacht is at anchor just inside the reef. The Lucky Tiger is 130 feet long and two stories tall, with tinted windows, an outdoor lap pool and a heliport on her front deck. She is the ultimate billionaire's toy.

David arrives at the tiki bar to the sound of Duke Hanna music playing. He orders a pina colada, then seats himself and watches as a mahogany yacht-tender launch docks at the end of Skeleton Bay's long wooden pier. A broad-chested man wearing a blazer and khaki pants climbs out of the launch and scrambles onto the dock. Another man of similar size, wearing identical attire, passes up a heavy-looking contraption, then shimmies up the dock's ladder. Together the men fold the object out into what appears to be a rolling chair.

Back in the launch, an Asian man wearing a white suit and Panama hat stands up, then teeters off balance. Two other boat passengers leap to their feet and stabilize him. Tony, walking past the bar with the phone glued to his ear, is shocked when he sees David.

"Mudder sick!" he exclaims in his island drawl. "Didn't she tell you to stay in the room?"

"No. Should I go back?"

"Too late. We'll have to roll with it. Stay where you are, and don't make any contact with the Rev. That's him in the white suit."

"Well, I wasn't planning on—"

"Don't talk to him. Don't even look at him," Tony warns. "Reverend Huracan is a suspicious man."

The strongmen lift the Reverend out of the boat and lower him into the chair. The remaining passengers clamber up the ladder, then the entourage proceeds toward the patio as if in formation. At front and center, Reverend Huracan is pushed by two tall and slender minions who are dressed in white jumpsuits and sandals. These two have curious pancake-pale complexions, thick eyeliner, and black angular hairdos. Leather satchels are slung over their shoulders. Behind them, the wide-chested men swagger with cold, expressionless gazes as David takes a sip of his dwindling pina colada.

"You'll be okay," Tony whispers.

Chapter 18
The Rev

The team wheel Reverend Huracan up to a reserved table as a server arrives with a roquefort pear salad and a pot of Lapsang Souchong tea. The henchmen wander to the side of the patio while the androgynous attendants take their places flanking the Reverend. A male attendant begins cutting the pear, while his female counterpart fusses with a serviette and tucks it into the Reverend's collar. Huracan just stares ahead vacantly.

The guy sure knows how to make an entrance, David thinks as he glances out to sea and finishes his cocktail. As directed by Tony, he doesn't make eye contact with Huracan, but his peripheral vison senses that the Reverend is staring at him. David decides that enough is enough. He gets up to leave, but inadvertently glances in the direction of the entourage and locks eyes with the cult leader. David feels paralyzed by the Reverend's intense gaze. It's as if

Huracan can see inside his mind. David struggles to remain calm, but almost jumps out of his skin when someone taps his shoulder from behind.

"Hey. Didn't I tell you to stay in the room?" Sophie says.

"Ah, no."

She leans in. "We have to get back. The less interaction here, the better."

David couldn't agree more, but he decides to level with Sophie about something that continues to trouble him.

"I hate leaving my ex in the lurch like this. Zeke is supposed to stay over, and Belinda is going out on some 'hot New Year's date'. It's going to be World War IV if I don't at least contact them."

"Done," Sophie replies. "Somebody's been in touch."

"Really? How did that go over?"

"Let's just say, it's a good thing you're several hundred miles away."

Just then, from across the patio, the sound of a gentle voice.

"Sophie? Is that you?"

"Reverend Huracan. It's been a long time," she replies, squeezing David's arm.

"Please. Come sit."

Huracan motions to a pair of open chairs on the opposite side of his table.

David is surprised that Sophie knows Huracan. As they walk over and seat themselves, he wonders if this might be a test, but feels confident with Sophie at his side. Huracan waves furiously at the bartender, who rushes to shut the music off.

Red flag, David thinks. *How could anyone not like Calypso?*

Reverend Huracan is a handsome man of Asian and South American descent. He is thin and young-looking for someone who must be close to sixty. His skin is pale and smooth and well cared for, but it seems to be uncomfortably tight, exaggerating a thin mouth and high cheekbones. His hands are disfigured, with pulled-in fingers that form a partial fist. David guesses that the Reverend must have some sort of crippling degenerative disease. His "chair" is really more of a throne, carved from exotic wood and encrusted in gold inlay. It is adorned with symbols that look to be megalithic-era Peruvian.

"Sophie. I haven't seen you in so long. I sense that life is well," Huracan says, his voice slow and indifferent.

"I've been off the island for several years now, Reverend. Studying in Paris. Although the word 'studying' may be an exaggeration."

Huracan laughs thinly, but his jumpsuited attendants retain an icy demeanor.

"And who is this handsome young man?" the Reverend asks.

"This is my fiancé, Davi—"

"David Smith, sir. Pleased to meet you." David reaches out to shake hands, but the female attendant lunges forward and grabs his arm. Even the gray-suited henchmen take notice and move in.

"Oh it's fine, Ariel. We can make an exception for this one. I'm most curious about him." The tall and slender beauty shows disdain toward David as she releases her grip, possibly even jealousy. Beneath her thick makeup, Ariel looks to be of South Asian descent.

Huracan leans forward. He studies David's face, then reaches for his hand and cradles it while staring into his eyes.

"Do you believe in fate, David?"

David finds this to be quite creepy, but he plays along, though realizing now why it may have been simpler had he stayed at the cabin.

"I'm not a religious man in a traditional sense," David confesses, "but yes, it seems obvious that there must be some sort of higher power."

Huracan's expression brightens. He seems impressed.

"Would you be averse to consulting the oracle? I sense much energy in you," Huracan continues. "I'd be interested in learning more. That is, if it's alright with your lovely fiancée."

Sophie maneuvers a careful response, but she knows better than to refuse Huracan's wish outright. It would be of great insult to a leader who wields considerable power.

"Oracle? I'm not sure what you mean, Reverend, but we're busy this af—"

"Well, if it'll only take a few minutes," David interjects, missing Sophie's lead, "then sure. I don't see why not."

Huracan releases David's hand. He turns to his male attendant.

"Ganymede. The coins."

A stone-faced Ganymede reaches into his side satchel and retrieves a thin wooden box. He places it on the table in front of David and lifts the lid. Inside it are three gold coins with square holes in the middle. Beside them, a black cup is covered in Asian calligraphy.

"The I Ching provides a surprisingly accurate connection with the Greater God," Huracan explains. "It has been called upon for millennia by emperors and kings. Historic battles have been predicated on its teachings, and its deceptive simplicity belies its divinity." Ganymede gruffly clears the area in front of David, knocking a water glass over in the process.

"I cast five of my daily throws this morning at sunup," Huracan says as Ganymede fidgets impatiently. "But I had an epiphany *not* to make my sixth and final throw. The message seemed unclear, but now I understand. The last throw was meant for you, David."

David glances longingly at Sophie.

"Oh, I don't know. These chance-of-fate games creep me out." David says. "I remember playing with a Ouija board when I was a kid. Swore I'd never do that again."

The Reverend smiles with fake sincerity.

"Simply place the coins in the cup, then shake them freely," he explains. "When you feel that time has reached a universal juncture, let the coins fall onto the table."

Sophie looks on supportively, but she clearly thinks this is a bad idea. She nods at David, who drops the coins into the cup and swirls them around. He covers the cup with his hand and shakes it up and down while staring intently at the sky. At what he feels is the perfect, synchronous moment, he lets the coins tumble out.

Ariel looks on with interest as a scowling Ganymede reaches over and arranges the coins into a vertical column. The grumpy-faced disciple takes out a rice paper pad, and using a tiny pencil, draws a series of solid and broken horizontal lines. After dividing the pattern in half then sketching two three-lined figures, Ganymede tears the sheet off and places it in front of Huracan, all the while staring coldly at David.

"The coins create patterns called hexagrams," Huracan explains while picking at his lunch, "and the I Ching produces a total of sixty-four. How they interact elucidates great detail from an omniscient power. And this... is a most interesting reading."

Huracan's thin lips form a tight smile.

David is tired of being centered out, and doesn't at all believe in what he considers to be charlatan mumbo-jumbo. Sophie, who knows a great deal about Huracan, and to David's surprise knows him personally, appears curious to hear the coins' interpretation.

"What does it mean, Reverend?"

Huracan glances up at his female attendant.

"Ariel, why don't you take this. Do you need to consult The Book of Changes?"

Ariel bows.

"Infinite praises, my All-Knowing Lord. I shall do so without the book. The first hexagram is number 49, or Ko, which signifies Youthful Foolishness. This shows the need for total transformation."

"Excellent," Huracan says, then takes a sip of Lapsang Souchong tea. "Go on."

"Forty-seven is changing into K'un, or Deepest Night of the Soul. No one is stronger than fate, and the superior man stakes his life on following his will."

"Excellent interpretation, Ariel," Huracan says. "Sophie. You must keep an eye on this one. He is strong-willed and driven, but his inner rebel leads him astray."

"I have to say, that is quite an accurate description," David says.

He looks over at Sophie, who raises an eyebrow.

Huracan suddenly grimaces and clutches his side. Ariel rushes up to him and signals Ganymede, who removes an oblong case from his satchel. At the same time, Ariel rolls up the Reverend's shirt sleeve, revealing an IV stent in the crook of his arm. Ganymede removes a pre-filled syringe from the case. After purging some tiny air bubbles, he secures the end of the needle into the receptacle.

"We must now end our social," Huracan whispers.

"I hope you're okay, Reverend," Sophie says. "We'll see you tonight. David will be performing with the band on a few songs."

But Huracan seems oblivious to his surroundings now. His eyes wander anxiously. Ganymede presses the plunger on the syringe and the Reverend jerks into his chair. His head falls back and his eyes roll skyward before his face relaxes and he slumps forward.

"Leave us!" Ganymede snorts, motioning furiously for Sophie and David to move on. Ariel glowers at them as they exit the patio.

When out of earshot, a hundred feet down the beach, David stops and faces Sophie.

"That guy is too intense! And what the hell was that injection?"

"Probably heroin, among other things."

"What about when I tried to shake his hand? Even those dead-eyed killer types in Hugo Boss moved in."

"That's because no one is allowed to touch him."

"Uh. Okay."

"The Reverend's followers believe he is a reincarnation of the ancient Mayan god Juracán, who first spawned humanity, then angered and took it away with a great flood," Sophie explains.

"Well," David says, laughing drily. "That's all rather intense. Next time you need a nap, try and brief me first?"

"Duly noted."

"So what's next on the agenda?"

"Scuba."

"Oh great. This day just keeps on getting better."

Chapter 19
Marlin Cay

Back at the cabin, David discovers a wetsuit laid out for him on the bed. He squeezes into the 5 mm O'Neill and finds that it fits perfectly. Sophie also changes into diving apparel, and David admires her athletic physique as he follows her out the cabin door. After walking past a shell garden toward the ocean, Sophie leads David through the crystalline shallows toward Skeleton Bay's pontoon boat. He's alarmed at how frigid the sea feels on his tender feet, but he hides it well. Drago helps them aboard, and with Mr. Pong at the helm they set off toward a tiny island a mile offshore.

As the boat cuts across the coral-specked bay, Drago outfits David with fins, a mask, a snorkel, and hands him an inflatable buoyancy-control vest called a BCD. The thought of going underwater is beyond terrifying for David, but at least he feels some relief knowing that Belinda and Zeke have been contacted.

In under ten minutes, they arrive at Marlin Cay, a weather-beaten atoll that is nothing more than a white sand beach surrounded by a tangle of battered vegetation. The southwest side of the island is sheltered and calm, but the north and eastern shores face the open Caribbean, where ocean waves crash on a coral reef as sharp as shattered glass. David guesses that for centuries ships have been steering clear of this beautiful but perilous cay.

Pong tilts the engine up and guides the boat in as close as possible to the sandy shore, where Sophie and David jump out into knee-deep water. With Drago's help, they grunt the diving equipment to the beach. After checking and confirming that both air tanks are topped up to 3,000 PSI (pounds per square inch) of air, Drago and Pong motor off, leaving Sophie and David on the tiny island paradise.

Alone together and surrounded by the crystal-blue Caribbean, David can't take his eyes off of Sophie. She is mysterious and desirable, and the two of them seem to share common personality traits. Sophie is confident, willful and strong, but at the same time has a delightful childlike spark. David, though mystified as to why he's here, has made a pact with himself to live for the moment and to roll with anything that might come his way.

"Do I really have to learn scuba?"

"It's going to be an intense night," Sophie says, a tinge of worry in her voice for the first time. "After completing our work at

Huracan's, an underwater exit may be the only way out of there."

"Night diving!"

"You'll be fine. Although we have a saying down here— dark and sharky."

"Thanks for that."

"If it makes you feel any better, there are just as many sharks out there right now."

"That's comforting. How do you know all this?"

"I grew up on Andros," Sophie says, before looking off to sea. "I was blessed with a mostly happy childhood."

David wonders what she means by "mostly", but now is clearly not the time for life stories.

Sophie helps David get suited up. She places his Buoyancy Control Device (BCD) and tank over his shoulders, tightens some straps, and clips the front of his vest together. David fights the urge to shout for the boat to return as she secures lead bars in pouches on his on his weight-belt. After some verbal instruction on the beach, they shuffle out of the shallows to shoulder-deep water. There, they go through scuba basics: controlling buoyancy by letting air in and out of the BCD, checking air gauges, equalizing ears, and the all-important hand signals.

Then they work through more advanced scenarios, like clearing a water-filled mask using air bubbles, recovering a lost regulator, and the counterintuitive technique of breathing from just a stream of bubbles, without a regulator. Gradually they ease into ten, then twenty feet of water, where they use a compass to navigate.

David is so challenged and excited that he soon forgets his fear. All the while, Sophie points out underwater sights, including a curious rainbow parrotfish sailing past, a pair of baby sea turtles fluttering by, and a cranky moray eel that peers up suspiciously from a nearby coral cavern.

They surface, and Sophie informs David of the next series of exercises, then they proceed to a depth of thirty feet, where they sit on the bottom amid a waving field of green seagrass. Sophie has David remove all his gear and then put it on again, a procedure called "ditch and don". After this difficult exercise, they practice emergency ascents and share a single regulator while performing "buddy breathing". Sophie nods, impressed by David's newfound level of ability and confidence—that is, until a six-foot-long reef shark meanders by, barely twenty feet away.

David points emphatically at the menacing creature. Sophie responds by making a pair of "okay" symbols using her thumb and forefingers. She points to her eyes with two fingers, the diving signal for "watch me." She unhooks a plastic bottle from her waist-belt and starts twisting it, which makes a scrunching sound. The shark seems to become hyper-aware. It twitches then moves in close, momentarily blocking

David's view of the surface as its sleek body glides over his head. Paralyzed with fear, David executes a perfect, primordial play-dead instinct and floats lifelessly beside Sophie. It's killing him to be so ignobly transformed into a feeble wuss, but he doesn't dare move a muscle as the torpedo-like creature passes between them and circles around, all the while keeping its prehistoric eye locked on David. Sophie crunches the bottle again, and a smaller shark darts behind her as the six-footer returns and bumps the bottle with its nose.

David inches his hand out from his chest and tips it back and forth, the universal signal for "diver unwell." He points upward with his thumb and Sophie nods. Slowly, they swim upward and surface. David pulls the regulator from his mouth and looks down past his fluttering feet, trying to locate the sharks that were there a minute ago.

"I think that's enough for today," he grunts.

Sophie reaches over and puts a puff of air into his BCD for floatation.

"You're a natural at this!" She exclaims, stretching the truth a little. "I think that was Sergeant Major. He's grown since the last time I saw him."

"You know the sharks by name?" David asks, his frown changing to a disbelieving smile. "It looked pretty hungry to me."

"He did seem to be eyeballing you," Sophie teases. "Reef sharks are well-behaved. It's those eighteen-foot hammerheads that make me nervous."

"That makes two of us."

Just then, a fifty-foot cabin cruiser rounds the far side of the island, piloted by someone high above the water in an outdoor cockpit known as a flying bridge. The boat turns their way, then slows as it approaches them.

"Someone you know?" David asks.

"Let me do the talking," Sophie replies.

An African-American crewman stares down at them from the back deck as the yacht's engine shuts off and it drifts over. David eyes Sophie, but he does as he's told and keeps his mouth shut. Besides, he keeps peering into the depths through his mask, looking for ravenous sharks.

"Find any conch today?" the crewman asks.

"Only the best kind for fritters," Sophie answers.

"My gran has an excellent recipe," the man counters.

"I'll be there with bells on," Sophie replies.

Without another word, the man walks astern, opens an outside door and folds a ladder into the water. Sophie motions for David to follow and they swim to the launch together. She clings onto the aluminum rungs and takes off her fins, then the sturdy crewman helps her aboard.

"Welcome aboard, Cap'n Bisset," he says as Sophie sloshes across the deck and starts removing her scuba gear.

The crewman throws her a towel, then turns toward the side of the boat where David, looking very alone and vulnerable, is anxious to get out of the sea. He reaches for the ladder, but the man pushes his hand out and signals for him to Stop. David looks up and notices a machine pistol hanging from the crewman's shoulder.

"No, no. You stay right where you are."

Chapter 20
Lady Argon

A voice calls out from the flying bridge.

"He's okay. Let him up."

The voice sounds familiar, but David can't place it. The crewman eases his threat level and helps David out of the water.

"Collins, take the helm. I'm coming down," the voice says.

"Yes, sir," Collins replies.

David looks up and sees someone stepping onto a ladder that leads to the bridge. Sophie seems completely unaffected by it all as she passes her towel to David and helps him wriggle out of his gear. Then the familiar-sounding voice speaks again, from just behind him.

"Welcome aboard, David."

David spins around.

"Ned McCarty!"

David is overjoyed. For the first time in nearly twenty-four hours, he's seeing a familiar face and, more importantly, the face of a friend. Ned from the Argon Electric store has been a mentor and guide through the world of electronics since David built his first bass amp when he was seventeen years old.

"So, you're behind all this," David says, grinning as they give each other a firm handshake. "I always suspected you were in this business."

Ned cocks his head to one side.

"Right. You can neither confirm nor—Never mind. You have no idea how good it is to see you, Ned. I've been alone in this shark tank for almost twenty hours now."

"That bad, eh?" Ned replies. "Oh well. You can't change the past."

McCarty is an intelligent-looking man in his fifties with salt-and-pepper hair, wearing navy slacks, a NASA windbreaker, titanium wire-rimmed glasses and a space shuttle Discovery baseball cap.

"You look great, Ned. The island lifestyle suits you."

"Thank you, David. Yes, it does. I had a three-hundred-pound marlin on the line this morning. But, as you obviously know by now, there's a bigger fish we need to bring in."

"Reverend Huracan," David replies.

"David's had a basic briefing, but no real details yet, sir," Sophie says.

"Thank you, Captain Bisset. Good to finally meet you. Why don't you two come in, warm up, and I'll tell you what we know to this point. Thank you for your service, David. I'm sure you're anxious to find out what your place is in all of this."

"Yes, sir. I am so ready."

"Collins!" McCarty shouts to his crewman, who is already up on the flying bridge, "Take us to BH 302. Cruising speed."

"Roger that."

The engines grumble to life and the yacht speeds toward the open ocean, leaving a massive wake behind them. Ned leads Sophie and David down a steep set of stairs into a cozy cabin equipped with a tiny kitchen and bench seating, then directs them toward a door at the front of the cabin. There, another armed guard stands aside.

"Watch your head here," Ned advises, pointing at a low door frame.

David feels warm air radiating out of the room as he squeezes in through the diminutive entranceway. When he looks up, he is dumbfounded. There are switches, dials, and numbered readouts everywhere. The long and narrow room is brimming with electronic equipment. One computer screen appears to show pathways of satellites orbiting Earth. Another monitor shows a topographic map of what looks to be the ocean bottom. There are blinking icons of all shapes and sizes scattered across the screen.

"Welcome to the Lady Argon. She's actually a mobile command center."

"Holy shit!" David exclaims.

Though Wesson doesn't particularly like the use of sentence-enhancing words, this control room is swear-worthy. To an electronics geek, it's like a roomful of presents on Christmas morning. Even Sophie seems amazed.

"Unbelievable, Ned. Is this all yours?"

"Thank you, Sophie. I built most of the equipment. David doesn't know it, but he's worked on a number of these components. Remember that modified PPG control board you fixed for me last March?"

"I do," David replies.

"It's in here."

"I figured it was for some New Wave band."

Ned points to a rack-mounted power head with sturdy metal handles on either side. The expensive-looking component is covered in flashing red-and-green lights.

"It's a naval positioning system. Let's see ..."

Ned flicks some switches, and a series of maps begin to appear on a television monitor above the device.

"Here's the Black Sea. And the eastern Mediterranean. Now here we are in the Caribbean. You get the idea."

"Is this us here?" asks David.

"It is."

David points to a cluster of icons on the map.

"What are those?"

Ned smiles, proud of his protege's observation.

"Those two cigar-shaped icons are submarines. Fortunately, one of them is a friendly. The other is a Soviet Akula-class hunter-killer that we've geotagged and are tracking. And they're both less than fifteen miles from here."

"Yikes."

"This is a sensitive craft you're on, David. If I were to send out an emergency signal, our friendly out there would instantly be put on high alert, and F-16s would be scrambled out of Homestead Air Force Base"

"So what does all of this have to do with me?" David asks.

"I thought you might ask," Ned replies. "Why don't you guys take a seat on the bench here. I'm going to fix us a cup of Bovril, then we'll proceed. Sound good?"

David and Sophie nod in agreement, then Ned exits the room, past the guard stationed outside the door.

"Oh, man. This is crazy," David says.

"You ain't seen nothin' yet," Sophie assures him.

Chapter 21
Cold Comfort

Ned and his below-deck crewman Fisher return with steaming cupfuls of the salty broth. David, fighting off a chill and eager to get some blood back into his fingers, wraps his hands around the covered cup. Fortunately, the Lady's control center is warmed by a multitude of glowing electronic devices, and even the rumble of her twin 1,000-horsepower Yanmar engines is strangely comforting as she propels them across the rolling Caribbean at twenty knots. The ride is surprisingly smooth, except that whenever the Lady's bow falls over cresting swells, one experiences a mild weightless stomach effect. After paging Collins and suggesting he slow down a tad, then organizing some folders at his workstation, Ned seats himself in a swivel chair.

"We're pleased to have you with us, David. You've long expressed interest in joining The Service, so it must feel strange being here now."

"Yes sir, it does."

"I'm going to start with the basics, then move into specifics, but first, some official requirements to tidy up." Ned hands David a stack of papers.

"Time to sign my life away?"

"Pretty much," Sophie assures him. "You're going to have an operation-specific tier-three clearance. For a newbie, that's substantial. And as you know, our governments have the discretion to deny all knowledge of our activities. Plus, you'll be agreeing that everything here is eyes-only classified."

"I've dreamt of being with the CIA since I was a kid."

"This isn't a CIA position," Ned clarifies.

"Oh?"

"My private contracting firm, Vector Frontline Systems, acronym VFS, has been conducting operations for The Five Eyes countries for over ten years," Ned explains. "Every one of them successful, I might add."

"Amazing. Congrats, Ned. I'd be honored to be part of it, but would love to understand what I'm getting into."

"Sign away, then," Sophie says. She hands him a pen.

David can barely contain his excitement as he endorses the required pages. Then, after a round of congratulatory handshakes, Ned gets down to business.

"What does David know about Huracan?"

He flips a switch, and a picture of the Reverend appears on one of the screens.

"David is aware that Reverend Huracan is a charismatic leader, with cult followers who believe he's a living god." Sophie explains. "But his main business is the illegal trafficking of sensitive missile and space technologies. His underground network has been smuggling out plans and components from a number of top-shelf military and civilian space projects."

Ned switches a picture of the space shuttle Columbia onto a monitor. "I know you're aware of the space shuttle," he says, "but you may not have seen the Russian version, the Buran Orbiter K1."

Ned splits the screen and loads up a picture of the Buran Orbiter.

"They're almost identical!"

"Huracan made a lot of money selling our plans to the Russkies," Ned explains, "but he's ticked them off by selling their components and plans to us."

"He's also in bed with the Colombian cartel," Sophie interjects, "and leases some of his considerable Bahamian land assets as transport hubs for cocaine distribution."

"The guy is into everything," David says.

"But now," Sophie continues, "even the Colombians are furious with him over some deal gone bad."

"He must have quite the death wish," David replies.

Ned and Sophie look at each other and their demeanor flattens.

"Herein lies the problem," says McCarty. "He does have a death wish, but unfortunately, not only for himself."

"Six months ago, we received intel that Huracan had taken possession of a weapon," Sophie elaborates. "One we are extremely concerned about."

Ned presses a series of buttons on the keypad and another image takes over the screen. The room suddenly feels drained of the almost euphoric atmosphere of the signing process.

"Oh, come on," David says.

"It's a heavily modified Pershing 1 missile," Ned explains.

"I don't even want to ask. What kind of warhead?"

"This unique prototype had a conventional, 1,000-pound payload," Ned continues, "but we believe it's been customized and fitted with a hybrid nuclear tip."

David feels for a moment like he's outside his own body. Perhaps it's a defense mechanism protecting him from thinking of the ramifications of such a device in the hands of a madman.

"Where the hell would he hide that?"

Ned loads another image onto the screen. It looks like an elaborate hand-drawn map.

"For over a year, we've been charting a cave system that occurs naturally under the ocean beside Huracan's compound," he says. "We think the missile is housed in this area here."

He points to a large open section.

"It's called a 'solution cave,' and it's big enough to hide a submarine."

"You think he has a sub in there?"

"Negative," Sophie says, "but one of our transport ships went missing last year— long story, I'm not going to get into it, but by the time we found and secured the vessel, one of her missiles had been removed."

Ned pulls up a satellite view of Huracan's property.

"We have credible intel that he's taken a land-based track, dropped it into the cave and created an amphibious silo. This heavy concrete dock acts as a bunker over a hidden launch array. The dredging and construction have taken place at night or underground, to avoid being spotted by satellite."

"What do you need from me?"

"Ever heard of the Nuclear Football?" Ned asks as he brings up a picture of President Ronald Reagan at a press event.

"See the man behind the President carrying that heavy-looking leather briefcase? Inside it, there's a control panel that allows the entire US nuclear arsenal to be launched. 'The Football', as we call it, is within a hundred feet of the President twenty-four hours a day, seven days a week, wherever he is on the planet. Think of it as a doomsday trigger.”

“Huracan has a similar device for his missile that he pilfered from the barge,” Sophie adds. “Once the missile is fueled, he can commence its launch sequence by simply opening the case, turning a pair of keys, punching an entry code, and pressing Fire. Without intervention or cross-checks by anyone other than his overzealous followers. More on that later.”

“So, your job tonight,” Ned continues, “is to get to the Football and swap out an essential circuit. That way, we will have control of the missile instead of Temple of a Greater God.”

David feels the color draining out of his face.

“You want *me* to modify the circuit?! Jeezuz, Ned. It must be heavily guarded. And it’s probably booby-trapped.”

“Yes on both counts. But we have an insider in Huracan’s camp. And Sophie, who has been planning this operation for months, can get you up close and personal.”

“How do you know so much about this so-called Football?” David asks.

“I built it,” Ned replies. “But I can’t get in there— I’m too well known by his network of spies. The biggest wild card? There’s a double agent who will likely be there tonight. He goes by the name, Ennio.”

“Ah. Him again.” David says. He glances at Sophie with deadpan eyes. “Surely you must have a capable agent who's actually trained for this sort of thing."

"We did," Ned replies, "but—"

"He took a sudden, early retirement," Sophie interjects.

"That's encouraging."

The ship's engine suddenly slows.

"Arriving at BH 302," a voice crackles over the loudspeaker.

Ned picks up a CB-style microphone.

"Roger that, Collins. Get as close to the wall as possible. You stay at the helm and Fisher will help with the dive equipment."

"Yes, sir."

"The di—" David catches himself. Now that he's an officially recruited agent, wimpiness is not an option.

"This won't exactly be a beginner sortie," Sophie explains, "so prepare yourself mentally for a hundred feet."

David doesn't react outwardly, but inside he's running scared. Ned takes his NASA windbreaker off, and underneath it he's wearing a wetsuit. Then McCarty, a man with a stiff and socially awkward manner, looks uncharacteristically wide-eyed.

"Now let's get some eyes on that missile!"

Chapter 22

Vader

On the back deck of the Lady Argon, crewman Fisher helps the team suit up, while David gets a briefing about diving at depth. Sophie explains how water quite literally squashes air, and how one breath at a sixty foot depth is equal to three at the surface. Because of this, a nervous beginner can quickly exhaust their air supply.

She reminds David that when surfacing, inhaled air expands, so the golden rule of scuba is: *never... hold... your breath.* Otherwise, the lungs can become distended and could even explode during an ascent. Also, air pockets that are trapped naturally within the ear cavities need to be equalized regularly. If not, eardrums become excruciatingly painful and could even implode. Sophie reminds David how to equalize their pressure by pinching the nose and blowing into it.

"We're now just south of Huracan's property," Ned announces.

He points to a nearby spit littered with gnarled trees and washed-up seaweed.

"It's on the other side of this point, a quarter mile to the north. The Greater God compound doesn't have eyes on us here, but we can't stay here long."

"You're sure he doesn't have cameras in those trees?" Sophie asks.

"Intel says no, but if he does, there's nothing we can do about it now," Ned snips, sounding a bit testy. "But he will be seeing us on radar, so *we* need to be in the water and the *Lady* needs to be out of here within ten minutes," he says, sounding annoyed with Sophie for questioning his pre-op intel.

Captain Sophie instantly recognizes that men like Ned don't like to think that someone else, especially a woman, might actually be smarter than they are. Being female in a male-dominated business, Sophie has dealt with this syndrome many times. But as a professional soldier who has led countless life-and-death missions, she logs Ned's snub and quickly puts it behind her.

"We're now circling above Blue Hole 302," Ned announces. "These underwater formations go down to almost five hundred feet, but we'll be exiting at ninety feet into the southeast side of the cave system."

David doesn't like hearing words like *ninety feet* and *cave*, but he keeps his emotions in check.

"We go in under a coral bridge," Ned continues, "then make our way north for two hundred feet in a channel known as Birch

Creek. That will bring us back up to sixty feet. David, always good to check your compass from time to time."

"Got it."

"Now, the next juncture can be confusing. At the end of Birch Creek, there's a two-way divide, where both openings look very similar. But we take the right-side opening. Understand? At the divide, go right."

"The left opening leads to a turtle sanctuary inshore," Sophie interjects, "but there are multiple pathways in there and it's easy to get lost."

"Understood," David confirms. "At the end of Birch Creek, go *right*."

"Before we leave the divide," Sophie adds, "we're going to stop, do an air check and turn our headlamps on." Crewman Fisher shows David how to power up the headlamp. "You've got a brand new tank with extra air, so your pressure gauge should now show 3,300 psi."

David checks the gauge and makes an "okay" sign, his hand trembling slightly.

"This is new for you and a few spots can get claustrophobic, so stay calm, breathe evenly and remember: don't ... hold ... your breath," Sophie says. "Then it's up and across to Drago's Cave. It's confined in there and we'll be on artificial light, so take it slowly."

"And don't put any air in your BC," Ned interjects, "or you'll shoot up too quickly.

When we reach the cave, we'll get out of the water. O2 levels there are fine for breathing off-regulator."

David's brain is starting to hurt from too many details, but Sophie keeps him on task. "We have equipment there and are hoping to get a view of Huracan's operation. Ned is going to conduct some tests so we know exactly what we're dealing with," she says.

"And just so you're aware, David," says Ned, "you're in excellent hands with Captain Bisset. She's been diving on Andros for most of her life. Plus, she has a Navy SEAL Master Diver equivalent. There's no better wing-lady on the planet."

"I'm all yours," David says, smiling at her flirtatiously.

Sophie rolls her eyes as she adjusts his snorkel. Ned finds nothing cute about the flirtation.

"Smarten up!" he snipes, understanding the importance of keeping David's sometimes wandering musician mind on point. David shifts back into mission mode and watches as Fisher attaches an underwater flare to his belt. "These emergency torches are activated by bending them quickly and firmly at the top." Ned holds a flare out and demonstrates. "But only use them if needed and always keep them at arm's length. They're composed of magnesium, which burns at an extremely high temperature underwater."

David feels a headache coming on. Information overload. Sophie's trained eye picks up on his attitude shift.

"You okay?" she says, looking him over closely. She hands him a water bottle. "Take a few sips. Important to stay hydrated."

"So everybody keeps telling me." David sucks some water from the bottle's straw and realizes that he is incredibly thirsty.

"There's one final piece of gear," Sophie says.

She holds up a diving knife within an ankle sheath.

"It's regulation. When we dive in an obstructed area." As Sophie straps the knife to David's shin, his mind flashes to watching the movie Thunderball with his dad—one of his rare fond memories of his father.

He snaps back to the present when he sees Fisher handing Sophie a speargun. David notices that Ned has one too. He decides to not attempt any mildly humorous, nervous wisecracks, like asking if they'll be spearing lobsters for dinner. Besides, he's doing everything he can to keep his head together, and they haven't even hit the water!

A voice crackles over the ship's loudspeaker. "*W395 ... W395 ... This is G7N, Falcon leaving nest. I repeat. Falcon leaving nest.*"

"We've got to get moving," Ned announces. "Huracan's people know we're here and they're sending out a patrol, so

Collins will take the Lady to a secondary location. At the end of the dive, we'll rendezvous with Skeleton Bay's pontoon boat. Resort guests dive here all the time, so it won't raise suspicion once this vessel leaves for the open sea."

Ned points astern, where David is surprised to see the resort's dive boat at anchor a hundred feet away.

"Once we're out of the cave," Sophie interjects, "look for her anchor rope at the top of the wall and we'll follow it up together. There will be a safety tank hanging at fifteen feet, where we'll make a ten-minute safety decompression stop. All good, David?"

"All good," David lies.

"Then put a few puffs of air into your BCD and follow me," Ned says. "Sophie will be behind you at all times if you need her."

"Let's do this!" David exclaims with as much bravado as he can muster.

He takes a test breath from his regulator, then follows McCarty toward the back of the boat. He's not used to the extra weight or walking in fins, and he waddles like an injured penguin as Fisher steadies him from behind. Ned makes some adjustments to his own mask, puts the regulator into his mouth, then leaps into the water, keeping his legs outspread in a walking stance. He plunges in, then spins around and motions at David, who chomps on the regulator and hobbles to the edge.

As David looks up, the pontoon boat comes into his field of vision. To his surprise, Mr. Pong is sitting amidships, smiling with cruel enjoyment at David's awkwardness. David reaches up and scratches his head with his middle finger raised at the big Samoan. Pong's massive shoulders shake with a disbelieving chuckle. He lies back on the boat's seat, and covers himself with a windbreaker.

Imitating Ned's technique, David leaps off the Lady Argon. He hits the water and sinks in a cloud of bubbles before bobbing up to the surface. Ned swims over and gives him an "okay" signal, and David responds in kind. Ned points down with his thumb, then reaches over and presses the top button of David's BCD. Air starts bubbling out of the vest's exhaust tube. As they slip beneath the surface, David hears a muffled splash behind him. He looks down and sees Sophie, already twenty feet below them, scooting by as if she might have been a dolphin in another lifetime.

David feels a surge of confidence at the sight of her. It's just a bit odd getting used to the constant, gurgling, Darth Vader breathing sound.

Chapter 23

Subterranean Foyer

David struggles to keep pace with Ned, who leads him toward a hidden crevice at ninety feet. David finds that being underwater is oddly dreamlike, as if everything is taking place in a strange kind of slow motion. He has trouble keeping his ears equalized, and as they pass through a thermocline at seventy feet, his regulator starts making a high-pitched wheeze on every inhale. These newfound challenges conspire to unsettle David, but he lets his mind drift into a state of calm.

The team pauses at the dark cleft in the wall, where Sophie checks David's air gauge. David points at his headlamp, but Sophie shakes her head. After a round of "good to go" hand signs, Ned swims into the murky opening. David glances up before following him and is suddenly struck by a dizzying, reverse fear of heights when he sees the ocean surface rippling ten stories above him. He vows not to look up again, since this unexpected bout of upside-down vertigo has hastened his already nervous breathing pace.

Ned leads David into the subterranean foyer, and barely five feet above their heads, a coral ceiling shimmers with a wash of bubbles. Ned motions toward a blueish patch of light thirty feet away. He pushes off and David follows him along the jagged passageway toward it. Once there, the team drops into a narrow fissure, which David assumes must be Birch Creek. This area is devoid of fish, unlike the reef at Marlin Cay, which was teeming with colorful beauties. Gradually, over a two-hundred-foot-long incline, they ascend to a depth of fifty feet, not even close to David's comfort zone. Ned glances back from time to time and now Sophie swims up beside David, her eyes sparkling with excitement at how well he is doing. She motions at him with double "okay" signs, then points at a stone-and-coral ridge that has two cave-like openings on either side of it. David remembers this from the briefing as the divide where they take the *right-side opening*. The team pauses for a safety check, and David is shocked to discover that over the last section alone, he's burned almost a third of his air.

They switch their headlamps on and enter the right-side passageway, where the team swims toward a five-by-five-foot vertical shaft with no natural light inside of it. Ned confirms that Sophie is in close proximity to David, then rises and disappears in a bubbly cloud. David positions himself under the jagged opening, and after glancing over his shoulder to make sure Sophie is still there, pushes off and swims upward, remembering not to inject any air into his inflatable vest. He rotates his head in an easy circular motion as he rises, and his headlamp illuminates the craggy surroundings. He brushes off a shudder of fear and follows Ned for another twenty feet, where the corridor widens. Sophie's lamp illuminates David's pathway from behind and it brings him great comfort to know that she quite literally has his back.

As he pushes through what he prays is the final stretch, David breaks through the surface. A pair of strong hands reach down and help him onto a ledge inside an illuminated cavern.

"Welcome to my cave, Mr. X. Now turn off light. You're blinding me."

David is overjoyed to see Drago, the man who only hours ago threatened to throw him from the plane. Perhaps it's the concept of meeting a fellow human under the sea, or perhaps David has been stricken with a severe bout of Stockholm Syndrome and has fallen in love with his captors.

Sophie rises from the water and pulls the regulator out of her mouth.

"Way to go! Do you feel okay?"

"Pretty good, thanks, but you were right, not exactly a beginner dive."

"Great job, David," Ned echoes in congratulation. "In retrospect, that was tougher than I recall, but I think it's important that you see exactly what we're dealing with."

The cave appears to be a hundred feet long and twenty feet high, but it's impossible to be sure since the furthest corners of it fade to nothingness. Electric lights throw a tapestry of shadows off aquamarine-colored stalactites, and scattered across a flat section covered in reddish sand are the now-opened khaki cases. At the north end of the cavern, a metal bench supports a stack of electronic devices and a rugged-looking television monitor.

"How'd you get this all in here?" David says.

"That would be me," Drago replies. "And Sophie helped a tiny bit."

"Are we on the other side yet, Drago?" Ned asks.

"Almost there, Commander McCarty."

The Slovenian fires up a noisy drilling machine that turns a metal shaft within a two-inch-diameter tube in the north wall.

"Huracan's cave is directly on the other side of us," Ned explains. "Once Drago punches through, we're going to push a camera in and get a view on the monitor here."

Just then, the machine spins up and winds down.

"We're in," Drago says.

He eases the drill bit out and Ned passes him a black rubber tube. Drago works it into the hole while McCarty powers up the TV monitor. A blurred image lights up the screen.

"Hold up!" Ned shouts. "Can you tighten that, Drago?"

Drago twists a dial and the image sharpens. Sophie and David watch as the camera pans along a dimly lit corridor. Down the center of the narrow chamber, a massive tubular object is laid out on a track that is surrounded by a half-dozen workers wearing orange hazmat suits. Judging by their comparative size, the object looks to be thirty feet long.

"Can you get in closer?" McCarty says, his voice cracking with excitement.

Drago twists another dial and the camera zooms in on a triangular cylinder that is detached from the upper end of the tube. Ned starts tapping buttons on a keypad.

"What are you doing?" David asks.

"Taking pictures!"

"What's the verdict, Ned?" Sophie asks.

"It's a heavily modified Pershing 1, all right. Now let's see ..."

Ned flicks some switches, twists a dial, and a ticking sound starts crackling out of a tiny speaker.

"Drago, can you push the Geiger probe in another inch or two?"

Drago grabs the tube and works it into the wall. The speaker comes alive with a torrent of radioactive clicks. Ned's brow furls.

"Yep. It's a nuke."

Chapter 24
No In-Between

A hush falls over the team as each one of them processes the bad news in their own way. David, though he's decided to no longer dwell on the past, wishes it was all a false alarm. His life has become one of extremes—from benign and dull routine to all danger and drama, with no in-between.

"In light of this," Sophie says, "it's imperative that we get back to the lodge immediately. David, I'm going to swap your tank out for a full one. The tide is turning, so it's going to take some effort getting out of here."

"He actually plans to launch this thing? What's his target, Ned?"

Ned seems paralyzed. He knows more than anyone the destructive magnitude of Huracan's armament.

"The Pershing 1 has a range of 450 miles," he says. "Florida's east coast is within that range."

David responds with a single word. "Fuck!"

"It's been modified for liquid fuel, which is good for us since we can control its thrust," Ned continues, "but liquid's a helluva lot more dangerous than solid. One spark and—"

"Mr. X, I could use opinion here," the East European interjects. "I make wireless feed to Lady Argon, but trouble with transmitter. You can check?"

David walks over and looks at the unit in question. He pops its top cover off.

"Do you have a test kit?"

"Absolutely," Drago replies.

He unclips a multimeter from a rack-mounted drawer and hands it to David, who checks the transmitter with a pair of metal probes. For the first time, David feels like he is being useful to the team, no longer just an anchor dragging them down. Drago returns to camera adjustments while Ned continues taking pictures that spit out of a militaristic-looking printer. He scours over each of the images before stuffing them into a waterproof folder.

David quickly identifies the transmission problem.

"There's a capacitor that needs swapping out. Do you have a C104-25? And you're using a surface antenna?"

"Yes and yes," Drago replies. "In bottom drawer, are extra caps and miniature soldering torch. I put antenna last week, but no signal in or out."

David follows a wiring conduit from the back of the radio to where it disappears into the wall.

"This might have something to do with it."

He holds up a frayed section of cable.

"Good thing I didn't throw you from plane after all, X."

The Slovenian retrieves the soldering torch from the drawer and tosses it to David. David twists the wires together, brushes a needlepoint of flame heat over them, and adds a dab of solder. He lets the connection cool, then wraps the wires in electrical tape.

"Guys, there are energy bars and water here," Sophie says while switching out the tanks. "Make sure to eat something and drink up."

"We need to be out of here in ten," Ned announces. "David. Get suited up. Okay?"

"Roger that," David replies as he tears into an energy bar. He finds the replacement capacitor, unsolders the old and secures the new into place. After re-testing the circuit, he shuts the component's lid.

"Good to go, sir."

"Excellent, thank you."

Ned types and the words *'W395 TO G7N CONFIRM MESSAGE RECEIVED'* scroll across the monitor. Sophie motions for David to join her at water's edge.

"I'll help you with the new tank. It's topped up with extra air, but keep an eye on your air gauge, especially when below fifty feet."

Sophie helps secure David's equipment. He squeezes back into his fins, then sits at the water's edge, his feet dangling into the water.

"As soon as I get a response, we're out of here," Ned announces. "Drago, time to gear up. Enough cave time for today."

"Planes. Caves. Nuclear bombs. Never beach time for Drago," the lanky Slovenian complains.

As David tries to distract himself from his fear of getting back into the water, he starts fidgeting with his emergency flare, fascinated that these torches actually burn underwater. He takes it off his belt to practice the ignition technique, but as he gently twists the top of the flare, it makes a loud fizzing sound and sparks to life. The resulting flash startles everyone, especially David. He drops the torch into the water and watches as it tumbles down a rocky step, then rolls to a stop on the flat section ten feet below him.

"Sorry, guys!"

"Careful with those things!" Drago says. "Magnesium burns at 2,500 degrees."

Sophie and Ned glance over briefly from the far side of the cave, but quickly return to discussing what are obviously the complex logistics of the mission.

"Somebody might step on it," David says.

"X! You worry too much. Anyway, time to get out of this wretched stink-hole."

David seems fixated on moving the torch. After all, it's barely ten feet below him and the visibility is clear, he rationalizes. Besides, he's feeling poached in his wetsuit and could use a cool down. He puts the regulator in his mouth, positions the mask over his eyes and lowers himself into the dark water. David leans forward and dips his head.

Below him, nestled between a shattered conch shell and some broken bits of coral, the glowing flare is eerily reminiscent of a stick of dynamite. It burns a strange greenish color and is shedding a plume of toxic-looking yellow smoke. David lifts his head and glances across the cave, but all three of them are engaged in conversation now. Not wanting to bother the team at this crucial juncture, David decides to move the torch.

He slips blow the surface, and making a classic newbie error, lets too much air out of his buoyancy-control vest, which sends him plunging with arms flailing. Thankfully, in barely a second, his feet land on the pebbled plateau, where they kick up a cloud of mucky silt. David secures a foothold as best he can on the slippery bottom, then takes a panoramic look around.

A shiver races up his back when he sees that he is surrounded by a totality of blackness, except for the sputtering light of the emergency torch at his feet. He takes a calming moment, knowing that at these depths, every urge to breathe must be controlled.

David tilts his head sharply to the left in hopes of equalizing his right ear, which has been a painful bother the entire dive. After a cold water trickle and a watery pop sound, the pressure normalizes, so David stoops down and picks up the flare. He looks up to find a place where no one will step on it and spots a suitable location fifteen feet away, but as he starts half walking, half swimming toward it, something *immense* moves out of the shadows in front of him.

At first it looks like a massive gray boulder, but when David holds out his flare, it illuminates a gaping-mouthed Nassau Grouper. The leviathan must weigh five hundred pounds. David feels tiny and insignificant in front of the giant creature. He channels his inner fish whisperer and waves the torch gently back and forth to encourage the beast to move on, but that only serves to threaten the cornered giant.

Without warning, it charges him.

A cloud of bubbles explodes out of David's regulator as the red-eyed behemoth rams into him with the force of a small car. The impact knocks the wind out of his lungs. He finds himself tumbling within a dizzying array of bubbles— downward and backward into nothingness. He slams into a coral abutment, where the magnesium torch is ripped from his hand. David reaches for it but the current surges, pushing him backward toward the void. He hears his headlamp scraping against rock and raises his hand to secure it, but winces as his knuckles drag across an outcrop of fire coral. David kicks with a Herculean effort and finally slows to a stop, but there's barely a toehold to hold his position here. He reaches up for his headlamp. It's gone.

He's so disoriented he has to watch his own bubbles just to confirm which way is up. The tide suddenly presses, and David sees his sole source of light receding as he drifts into the darkness behind him. He stretches every fiber out to retrieve the torch, but it's already out of reach. Then, just before being sucked into the ink black cave system, a fortuitous lull in the current allows him to break free of the water's terrifying power. It takes a superhuman effort to avoid getting dragged away, but he's finally able to snatch the flare from the ocean bottom and swim behind the shelter of a limestone wall.

David holds the sputtering torch up to get his bearings, but now, nothing looks familiar. Everything in every direction looks the same.

Never before has he felt so alone.

Chapter 25
Unearthly Shadows

David slows his breathing, remembering that at sixty feet below, every nervous breath is equivalent to three at sea level. If the ocean's surface were visible, he could ascend and break through it easily, but above him now, unearthly shadows dance across a low coral ceiling, animated by the light of his undersea torch.

At best, the flare has ten minutes left before it fizzles out, so finding the headlamp is paramount. His mask is almost completely fogged up, but he's too scared to clear it by letting a controlled amount of seawater rush in. So David tips his head forward and swishes the water already inside his mask. His pressure gauge appears to show under 2,000 pounds, but it's impossible to be sure in the greenish glow of his torch.

He attempts to retrace his path against the current, scouring the pebbled floor for his lost headlamp. Then twenty feet ahead, on a rock-strewn area, David spots a glint of light. He kicks toward it, but it's just a reflection from a piece of abalone shell. Then he sees something waving in the current on a branch of coral.

The headlamp!

He swims over, untangles it and flips the switch, but nothing. David discovers that although the lens has been shaken loose, the bulb looks intact. It's awkward holding the burning torch without melting his wetsuit, but he dares not put it down, terrified of snuffing out his only working light source. David gently twists the headlamp's lens a quarter turn and is rewarded with a blaze of light. Feeling an uptick of confidence knowing his odds of living just went up, David re-fixes the life-giving lamp on his head and swims toward an opening that is sparkling with turquoise illumination.

Maybe it leads to the surface, or back to the equipment cave, he thinks

Wherever it goes, it's the first sign of hope he's encountered. His flare continues to weaken. Soon it will expire. David positions himself under the open mouth and fights to maintain position in the ever shifting current. He drops the dying flare and starts ascending, taking utmost care not to crush the headlamp on a rocky outcrop above him. The passageway begins to narrow uncomfortably, but he suppresses a wave of claustrophobic panic and pushes through it.

After squeezing through another alarmingly tight section, David enters an illuminated cave that is filled with stalactites and schools of fish. He looks up, full of hope, but is devastated to discover that the light is emanating from a two-foot-wide crevice that is too narrow to swim through. Above it, angry waves are thundering. When David collided with the giant grouper, he must have tumbled into the left-side entranceway, the one everyone told him to avoid.

For the first time in his life, David begins to question his own mortality. He adjusts for neutral buoyancy and floats in the middle of the luminous cavern, surrounded by ancient rock and coral formations.

I must be so close to the cave. Maybe they're still there. If not, at least there's oxygen and I could send out a Mayday, he thinks, but when David looks around, he can't even locate where he entered this part of the cave. He feels intensely alone. His sole companion is the gurgling sound of his regulator, reminding him with every breath that he's running out of air. Memories of his son start flooding David's thoughts.

What a stupid way to die.

Chapter 26
A Flicker Of Hope

David's only hope of survival will be to find a shore-bound passageway. Using his compass, he navigates toward the west wall of the cave, where he searches up and down in a grid pattern. He swims as high as fifteen feet below the surface before running into yet another coral roof.

Dammit!

At least at this shallower depth he can conserve some air. But when David checks his pressure gauge, he's alarmed to discover that it reads under 1000 pounds, meaning two thirds of his air is gone. Plus, he's left his headlamp on, needlessly draining its battery. There is no more room for error, not if David Wesson wants to live longer than the next twenty minutes.

As he shakes off a shiver of depressive hopelessness, a flicker of light catches his attention. A tiny object is moving above him in an easterly direction. This minuscule sparkle is followed by another. David swims closer and spots a pair of baby sea turtles, their feet fluttering instinctively toward the open ocean. He all at once remembers that during the briefing, there was mention of a turtle sanctuary inshore.

David looks back, following the creatures' vector and sees a six-foot-wide opening in the wall. There is no natural light inside of it, but David peers in from a distance and his headlamp illuminates a jagged, tube-like corridor. *It must be the way to shore.* He wishes there was another option, for once he enters this unforgiving passageway, he will be embarking on a one-way journey. In there, the current will be overwhelming, making a return impossible.

David closes his eyes and whispers his prayer. He says a thank you for his family, then positions himself in front of the dark, open hollow. He feels the insidious power of water pushing, then sucking him in.

David shoots into the twisting tunnel. Terrified that his regulator will get torn from his mouth, he forces his hand up under his chin and clenches his jaw. He tries to calm his racing heart, knowing that panicking here means death. The passageway suddenly angles sharply downward. David's ears feel like nails are being driven into them. He pinches his nose and grinds his teeth to equalize them as his depth gauge plummets.

Forty feet … Fifty feet …

He forces the regulator into his mouth. Without that, *at least it would be over fairly quickly*, he thinks.

Sixty feet. Seventy feet …

Fighting almost total disorientation and a sudden wave of nausea, David starts tumbling head over fin in the darkened chasm.

Oh God. Don't let me throw up!

A curious wave of warmth suddenly washes over him. David will later learn that he is experiencing a syndrome known as hyperoxia, or too *much* oxygen in the body. It's not an unpleasant feeling. In fact, it's verging on euphoric.

As he battles the sudden urge to sing a drunken sea shanty, David pops out of the chasm into a wide-open area, where the pleasant, woozy feeling is usurped by one of alarm. Above him, waves are thundering through splintered cracks in the coral, but there's still no way out. As he struggles to cling to any semblance of hope, David hears a sound:

Ping ... ping ... ping...

Probably some buoy on the surface, he thinks.

Then he hears it again, another series of three pings. Maybe someone is looking for him, signaling him. He reaches back and bangs on the tank with his fist, but can't make a sound through its stiff nylon cover. Then he remembers the diving knife. David unsheathes it from its ankle strap, strains his arm around and clangs his tank three times with it, then listens. Three pings ring out again. They sound faster in pace. He strikes the tank four times and is answered with four clangs. Someone *is* looking for him.

He checks his compass and follows the westward wall up with his eyes. Thirty feet above him, a flashlight beam. He scoots upward toward a keyhole-like opening. On the other side, there's a face. David feels tears welling. He shouts her name in his head.

Sophie!

Chapter 27
Intimately Close

Sophie points to David's air gauge, which now shows under 400 pounds. With a reading that low, David should already be topside, but the opening here is too narrow for him to swim through.

Sophie flashes an Okay sign, then motions for him to remove his buoyancy-control vest. David understands. He will have to squeeze through without his tank and regulator. Thankfully they practiced the ditch-and-don procedure at Marlin Cay, but it was difficult even while sitting on a patch of waving seagrass. David starts removing his vest, but has trouble maintaining neutral buoyancy. It's exhausting kicking to prevent himself from tipping upside down. Sophie motions at his weight belt, which will also have to be removed at exactly the right moment. Otherwise, he'll sink to the bottom or conversely, shoot upward.

She reaches through the opening and grasps David as he struggles to free himself of the awkward equipment. Sophie suddenly motions 'Stop'. She points to her eyes and places her hand on her regulator, then pulls it from her mouth and points it toward him. David understands: They will share Sophie's air the rest of the way.

He slides his buoyancy vest out onto his right shoulder as she loosens his weight belt. One slip-up will mean disaster. Sophie holds up a finger, then takes a breath and holds it. She passes her regulator to David, who removes his mouthpiece and takes two breaths from hers. He holds the second breath and passes her air source back to her while exhaling a tiny stream of bubbles the way she taught him back at Marlin Cay.

They repeat the process, but when Sophie passes it a third time, *three ... two ... one...* she counts with her fingers. She opens her hand and David ditches his vest. It spirals off, free-flowing in a storm of bubbles. At the same time, Sophie unclips David's waist clasp and releases his weight belt. It plunges into the blackness beneath his feet. He feels his pulse quickening as they grip each other's forearms. Sophie motions for him to swim through the crevice. David takes a last breath, passes the regulator back to her, then claws his way through the keyhole. When he reaches the other side, Sophie passes her air back to him. They cling to each other for a moment, their bodies close, then she motions toward a bluish opening a hundred feet away. They set off and swim toward the light while breath-sharing. Sophie indicates with her hand that they will pass through the opening, then she makes a cheering gesture. In words, they are *so close.*

They pass under the final coral bridge, and for the first time since following Ned into the cave system at ninety feet, David is greeted by a heavenly shimmer of open water above his head. Sensing him about to bolt, Sophie flips her hand up. She points to her watch, then holds five fingers up twice. David understands. They will conduct a ten-minute decompression break here. He's seen enough Jacques Cousteau specials to know that this is a safety measure. The last thing David needs after enduring such unimaginable terror is a case of the bends— a potentially life-threatening diver's condition.

They float together sharing Sophie's air, and ten minutes can't pass fast enough. She finally raises her thumb and they begin to ascend together, but David breaks away and swims upward at full tilt. He bursts through the surface and takes in a lungful of humid Caribbean air. Sophie breaks through a moment later. She pulls the regulator from her mouth as David punches his fist into the air, amazed to be alive.

A smile radiates across Sophie's face as they float on the surface of an inland blue hole that is surrounded by dense jungle vegetation. She looks over at David, who has his head tilted back and a serendipitous smile on his face.

"Okay, Mr. Wesson. You've got a lot of explaining to do."

Chapter 28
One Last Tear

"I'm so sorry," David says. "I never should have gone after the flare. A gigantic grouper rammed me and I got lost."

"No. It's my fault," Sophie replies. "I should have never taken you in there. We searched for you, then I came inshore as quickly as possible, figuring you must have drifted into Turtle Alley."

"Thank you for finding me. I wasn't ready to die."

"We got lucky. Pray it continues."

David follows Sophie to the south side of the lake and they clamber onto a floating dock.

"I have to check something. Can you gather the scuba equipment?" Sophie says.

"Sure."

As David organizes the gear, he is overcome with a surreal feeling, like the whole thing was a terrible dream. But he pushes his fear into the past where it belongs, and relishes the sound of birds chirping, tree frogs grunting, and wind whistling through the Caribbean pines. The calmness lasts but a few delicious seconds before a harsh reality creeps into David's thoughts. Tonight's mission is nearly upon them. He still needs so much more information.

"I hope Ned knows how to find this control box. Will he meet us at the lodge, Sophie?" David looks over his shoulder and sees her kneeling in the forest, back turned toward him, her head hung down in front of her.

"Sophie!"

David rushes over and finds her crouched in front of a rock-and-seashell arrangement that is surrounded by a bed of yellow elderflowers.

"Are you okay?" he says.

Sophie raises a hand and hides her face. With her other hand she waves him off. That's when David sees that she's crying. He sits softly beside her.

"I'll be fine," she says, her voice cracking. "It's just that ... I haven't been here in a long time."

"What's wrong?" David asks, all at once noticing two wooden crosses in the middle of the clearing. Sophie tries to regain her composure, but she's quivering and having trouble speaking.

"My mom and brother... drowned in that cave."

"Oh God. I'm so sorry."

"Little bro got pulled through that opening by an outward storm surge. Mom went after him, then Dad. I begged to go, but Dad wouldn't let me. And only he made it out, barely alive. Without them." Sophie's voice falters. "A recovery team discovered their bodies a week later, still clinging together. I think she must have found him, and died of a broken heart. He was Mom's fav—"

David places his hand tenderly on Sophie's shoulder.

She looks up at him with misty green eyes as he brushes a tear from her cheek.

"But you still went in there to save me," David says. "I owe you my life."

Sophie suddenly lunges forward. Her lips meet David's and she kisses him deeply. David feels his whole world melting away. He wraps his arms around her and pulls their soaking wet bodies together as her fingers glide down the side of his stubbled cheek. Maybe it's a moment in time that will never be repeated, but at this point, what else could possibly matter? Something about Sophie just feels right.

After their fleeting tender moment, they slowly untangle.

"Whoa. I'm not sure where that came from," Sophie says.

"Me neither, but *wow*!" David says, wide-eyed with disbelief. "Probably better if I remain speechless, or I'll end up saying something stupid." His clumsy words make Sophie smile as he brushes one last tear from her cheek. "Can't say I understand, but there's something different about you. I mean, I could see myself fa—" David catches himself. "See? This is what I'm talking about!" Sophie gives him a playful push. As David falls back, he pulls her with him. She ends up on top and they kiss again, entwined in each other's arms and legs.

The unexpected bliss is extinguished by the crescendoing thunder of an approaching helicopter. In seconds, the massive helo is hovering barely fifty feet above them, its deafening downwash kicking up dirt and debris.

"Talk about a vibe killer!" David shouts.

He covers Sophie protectively and shields her eyes.

"Who the hell is that?!"

"That," says Sophie with a mischievous smile, is our ride home: Ruthie 2."

"Ruthie 2? Girl, you never cease to amaze me!"

David laughs in disbelief until he looks up and sees the chopper's pilot staring down at him, wagging a finger.

"Gilbert?"

"Yup," says Sophie. "And I had to wake him from his afternoon nap, so he's going to be grumpy."

David gestures at Gilbert with an innocent shrug. He mouths the word 'sorry'.

Gilbert frowns, then he nudges the helicopter forward and starts landing it on a flat area two hundred feet away. Sophie and David dust themselves off and gather the scuba gear, but Sophie pauses for a moment and returns to the family memorial. David gives her some alone time as she clears away the debris. She bows her head in solace for a moment, then turns and hurries past him.

"Come on!" she says. "Let's go."

"Never a dull moment around here," David outwardly complains, but inside, he's *never* felt happier to be alive.

Chapter 29
A Living God

At first glance, Reverend Huracan's oceanside estate is a tranquil paradise adorned with manicured gardens, palm trees, and row upon row of purple bougainvillea. Multiple white cabins with red clay roofs are connected by forested pathways, and the Reverend's super-yacht, the Lucky Tiger, is moored at the end of a lengthy concrete pier. But beneath this idyllic veneer, there lies a rancid core.

There is a constant rumble from two pumping stations that spew diesel fumes day and night. The fifty or so above-ground inhabitants wear identical white jumpsuits and sandals, and all have the same haircut: crudely hewn with abnormally high bangs. A two-story clapboard barrack houses men on one side, women on the other, and at the center of the structure, Huracan's lavish suite features a circular bed built for five.

A dozen or so children are housed in a separate building, where they are raised and indoctrinated by strict custodians. The young ones have no contact with their parents, even though they live on-site in close proximity. A level below the luxurious upper suite, Huracan's war room is modelled on Louis XIV's parlor at Versailles. Here, the Reverend sits atop a throne in front of his highest-ranking disciples.

"Tomorrow is the end of beginnings," Reverend Huracan evangelizes. "And you, my devoted disciples, shall soon be gods. Olympus will pale in comparison to the dynasty of Huracan. I shall give you continents to rule. I shall ordain constellations in your likeness. What's left of humanity shall whisper only..."

"Huracan!" the disciples chant in unison.

"I trust the divine vessel shall be ready, Ganymede?"

"My Reverence, some of the workers, led by Professor Stonewall, have refused to complete their work, but we still hope to greet the sky at sun-up."

"Hope?" Huracan cocks his head.

"It shall be as you desire, Lord."

"Desire. Hope. How you disappoint me with such words, Ganymede. You have brought the saboteur to me?"

"Of course."

A door slides open and a worn out man wearing an orange hazmat suit stumbles in. His hair is matted, his face stained with oil. A disciple shoves him and he crumples to the floor. The man rises to his feet and faces Huracan.

"You have disobeyed me. What have you to say?"

"Lord, you promised to release me last week so I could reunite with my son. I have fulfilled my obligation to you and seek to return above ground to be with him."

"Obligation? That's all I am to you?"

Professor Stonewall falls to bended knee before his leader. "Of course not, Immaculate One."

"Where is this son of his?" Huracan grumbles.

Ariel enters the war room, holding an eleven-year-old boy coarsely by the collar.

"This is the boy," the disciple announces.

"My son!" Stonewall cries out. "Are you okay?"

The boy nods, but his eyes are fearful.

"He's a good, strong boy," Huracan says in a softer tone. "Do you love your son?"

"Oh yes, Lord. More than anything," Stonewall replies.

"So you love him more than you love *me?!*"

"Of course not, Your Reverence!"

Huracan turns toward the boy. "And what of you, boy? Am not I your true father?"

"But Lord—" Stonewall exclaims.

"Silence! He can make up his own mind. Let him choose. Ariel, release him."

Ariel releases the boy. He rushes toward his father, but a disciple grabs his arm. The lad fights hopelessly to break free.

"The choice is yours, professor," Huracan says. "If your work is not soon completed, the boy will become legally mine. And you ... shall be banished. Or worse!"

Stonewall falls into a worship pose.

"Thank you, Great Lord. I shall fulfill my duty."

A sliding door opens and one of the Reverend's gray-suited henchmen, enters the room. Audrius is extraordinarily wide chested and looks to be made of solid muscle. He nods purposefully at Huracan.

"You are fortunate, professor. I am feeling generous today," the Reverend says. "No. More. Delays. Now all of you– *Leave me!*"

Ariel and Ganymede walk to the front of the chamber and stand aside Huracan as the disciples bow and exit the war chamber, shoving Professor Stonewall and his son in front of them.

Audrius walks to the back of the room and inserts a key into a metal fixture. He twists it, and a panel rumbles open, revealing a polished golden elevator that is engraved with Mayan symbology. The four of them enter it and descend to a sub-level, where they exit into a starkly lit tunnel that slopes downward toward the ocean. Light bulbs hang every fifty feet from a twisted ceiling cable, and the passageway's walls are lined with ducting and pipes. Ariel and Ganymede offer to assist the Reverend as he hobbles toward an electric buggy, but he angrily brushes them off. After Huracan seats himself on the front passenger side of the transport, Ariel drives and Ganymede rides in the back, while Audrius swaggers behind them on foot.

The air is stiflingly hot, and soon there is an overpowering chemical smell. Huracan reaches for an oxygen mask as they pass a group of sickly-looking women and men who are staring out from behind steel bars.

"Lord!" a woman cries out. "Please. We need water. Food."

"You know better than to address me directly," Huracan replies without even a glance. "You'll have your water when it is ordained."

Ariel stops the buggy. She walks to the back of the vehicle and retrieves a pair of water jugs, then passes them through an opening in the cell door. More people arrive at the entranceway, all of them filthy and emaciated. They heap loving praises on Huracan, but he doesn't seem to hear them. Audrius walks into a darkened area, where he punches a numeric code into a keypad affixed to a rock wall. He unlocks another panel, flips a switch, and a partitioned metal door starts ratcheting up with a clattering sound. The disciples follow Huracan into a cavernous chamber.

Positioned down the center of the chamber, in a semi-assembled state on a rusted piece of railroad track, is the enormous missile. Orange-suited technicians are gathered around it, including Professor Stonewall who has just returned from his tribunal. The menacing-looking warhead lies detached from its olive-drab fuselage like a severed head, and another section near the top is splayed open, revealing a tangle of electronic circuitry.

Huracan's face reddens.

"Why is this not in launch position?!" he screeches.

"We had to make many modifications, Lord. Most of it had to be rebuilt to fulfill your specifications."

"Is the warhead armed?"

"Not yet, Excellency. It will self-arm when it reaches twenty thousand feet."

"You shall arm it immediately or sooner! Disappoint me again, professor, and I will detonate it right here!"

"It will be done exactly as you say."

Huracan, suddenly pale and drained of energy, turns toward Ariel and Ganymede.

"And another thing," he says, "This woman Sophie Bisset and her so-called fiancé? They are trouble. And they've been snooping around. I don't want either one of them leaving here tonight. Understood?"

Ganymede bows.

"Many praises, my All-Knowing Lord. Their death shall be my honor."

ACT THREE

Chapter 30
Last Details

The New Year's Eve sun is sinking at Skeleton Bay. It's the last of 1993, but hopefully not the last of a world that once was. Gilbert, despite being interrupted from his nap to pilot the chopper, has managed to prepare David an outfit for the Breakwater Mansion show.

"Looking quite dashing there, Mr. Wesson," Sophie says as David examines himself from every angle in the cabin mirror.

"Thank you, Mrs. Wesson. First time in Armani. I can see what all the fuss is about now. And *who* are you wearing? You look luscious."

"Easy now, big boy. We're not even married yet, but thank you. It's a re-creation of Grace Kelly's dress from To Catch A Thief."

"I don't suppose it's possible to share an enchanted evening under the stars, without all this save-the-world business?" David says.

"Ah, no." Sophie squeezes in and dominates the mirror. "We'll get the job done, and hopefully there'll be a tomorrow for us to celebrate."

"So how do you know this nutcase?"

"Years ago, my family went to church on the island, where Huracan was a junior minister. Except his name then was Nathaniel Klement."

"Before he rebranded himself as a living god?"

"Precisely. Nathaniel's the illegitimate child of a Nazi war criminal who was hiding in Argentina during the fifties."

"Some choice lineage there."

"Nathaniel took over the chapel when our beloved Father Gregory hanged himself in an apparent suicide."

"*Apparent* suicide?"

"Exactly my view, but murder was never proven."

Sophie holds up a pair of necklaces and models them both. "What do you think?"

"Definitely the first one," says David as he struggles with his tie.

"Good taste, Wesson. By the time Nathaniel took over the parish, he'd hooked up with major Colombian coke dealers. And so began his climb into money, weapons, and power."

"And protection from the cartel, I suppose. Can you help me with this?"

"That's when the cult began," Sophie says, as she fusses with David's Hermès tie. "A number of church members started making a *lot* of money. Nathaniel reinvented himself and opened the temple in Miami. There. I think that's got it."

"Where he came up with this whole Mayan god thing?" David asks as he checks his reflection yet again. "Oh yeah, that's perfect. Let me guess. He transitioned into money laundering."

"Big time," Sophie says, then she steps back. "David Wesson. You look fan-tastic."

"And you ... smashing, my dear," David replies, channeling his inner Cary Grant.

"By the way, this cover story of ours?" David says, his tone suddenly cocky, " This cover of ours, 'Mr. and Mrs. Smith'? Not good."

"What are you talking about?"

"You didn't know there's a Hitchcock film by that name? They were spies, I think. Someone should do a remake of tha—"

"It's only one night. Anyway, we better get moving. Oh! I almost forgot." Sophie rushes to her suitcase and returns with a baby-blue chiffon scarf. She drapes it over her shoulders and spins around in front of David. "Well?"

"You look like a goddess," he gushes. "But don't let it go to your head. We don't need any more deities around here."

"Piece of cake."

David marvels at Sophie's mixed combination of innocence, deadly precision, and confidence. She puts her arm in his and they exit the cabin into a gentle twilight breeze. The evening is body-temperature warm, the surf glinting off the last fingers of daylight as the elegant couple stroll down a palm-treed pathway. They soon arrive at the lodge's sport kiosk, where Tony is organizing life jackets, kayaks, and other inventory.

"Where's the red carpet?!" Tony exclaims when he spots them. He opens a side doorway. "Come in, come in. Quickly," he whispers.

Tony leads them to the far end of the counter, where he pushes some wetsuits out of the way, uncovering a hidden doorway. He raps on it three times, followed by two knocks in quick succession, and a reinforced portal creaks open. Tony holds Sophie's hand as she steps across the threshold in her Manolo Blahnik heels. David stoops to get through the entranceway, and they enter a seating area attached to a long and narrow hallway that is padded with soundproof insulation. David recognizes the room's purpose instantly. It's a shooting range.

"Good God, X! I thought it was a big curtain for you. That is how you say?"

"Close enough. Nice to see you too, Drago."

"You gave us a real start there, David," a second voice says.

"Sorry, Ned. I screwed up. Hopefully no more scuba."

"No more underwater adventures, God willing," McCarty says. "Good to see you."

Ned walks over and gives David a firm handshake. David attempts to pull him in with his signature one-armed hug, but Ned stiffens from his human interaction phobia.

"Enough of this lovefest," Sophie says, switching to all-business and slagging Ned at the same time.

Ned pushes David away and brushes himself off.

"You'll be sitting in with the band for a couple of songs," he explains. "We had someone out at your shows and apparently you know the repertoire."

"The tunes won't be a problem," David assures him.

"You'll be playing an all-'80s set," Sophie adds.

"Eighties? Somehow I can't picture Huracan being a Flock of Seagulls fan."

"Actually, he hates music," Sophie explains. His gathering get to hear it just once a year, on New Year's Eve, so they might go a bit nuts. At midnight, your set will be over. Huracan will take the stage and make a long-winded speech that usually lasts for hours, sometimes days,"

"Don't worry. I'm an expert at skipping the speeches."

"That's when you'll swap out the circuits. Sophie will get you where you need to go. Now, come here and take a look at this."

Ned leads David to a beaten-up road case at the far side of the room. David unclips its latches and lifts the case's lid. Inside, there's an electronic instrument with a four-and-a-half-octave keyboard and a silvery top populated with black knobs and buttons.

"It should look familiar," says McCarty. "I sent one to your house for repair."

"Ah yes. The OB-X synthesizer. By the way, that so-called 'customer' of yours? Not much of a personality."

"That's why he's so good at what he does," Ned replies. "He's one of my most trusted agents. Anyway, come see. When you open the top, the electronics look stock," Ned explains, "but when you flip up the main panel, there are two extra circuits beside the VCA."

David opens the keyboard and eases the main board up.

"Whoa. A lot of gold in there. What's that IC?"

"It's a clone of the Soviet SV-335 chip. You might remember we discussed it at the store."

"The one 'harvested from a UFO', worth ten million bucks."

"This is a reverse-engineered version, valued at five hundred thou."

"Seriously?"

"We built an entire factory in the jungles of Costa Rica to manufacture that little beauty. I'm the last to buy into this 'alien' business, David, but this circuitry is fifty years beyond anything I've seen."

David reaches inside the keyboard, squeezes the chassis' edges, and a six-inch-long electrical board pops out.

"You'll slip the circuit into this belt that goes under your shirt," Sophie explains, holding up what looks like a stretchy athletic back brace.

"So this goes into Huracan's control briefcase?"

"Actually," Ned exchanges an awkward glance with Sophie. "We can only now give you full disclosure, David. The circuit goes into the guidance system... of the missile."

Every muscle in David's body tightens.

"The missile? In the cave?"

"Correct. And there's a second location, where you'll swap the second circuit into Huracan's control briefcase."

David's head falls forward. The last thing he needs is to have face time with a nuclear warhead, in a horrifying cave, surrounded by rocket fuel, cult members, and dead-eyed security goons. But after snapping the circuit out, he turns and solemnly faces Ned.

"Whatever you say, boss. What about tools?"

"In the back of your stage amp," Sophie interjects, "there's a miniaturized tool kit that you'll slip into this pocket here."

"But how do we find th—"

"Captain Bisset knows that compound with her eyes closed. She's been on this operation for over a year. Plus, we have someone on the inside. It should all go very smoothly. Put your trust with Sophie, your faith with God."

David secures the components back inside the synth and closes it up. Sophie undoes his shirt, secures the brace around his lower back, then buttons him back up.

"If you get searched, you've got a bad back, right?"

"It's killing me."

The door squeaks open, and a man wearing a tweed jacket with breeches and a cap hobbles through the doorway. He's carrying a rectangular case.

"Sorry to wake you from your nap, Gilbert."

"Oh, not a worry, young man," Gilbert replies. "It sounded rather important. Plus, I hadn't flown Ruthie in quite some time. Sorry to be so tardy, but there's one more piece of equipment for you. It's rather heavy."

David takes the case from Gilbert and sets it down. When he opens it, his eyes light up.

"Whoa!"

David lifts out a futuristic-looking bass guitar. It has a beveled body with no visible headstock or tuning pegs.

"Always wanted a Steinberg bass."

"Well, it's slightly modified," Gilbert says. "If you flip this lever with your baby finger— Ah, you might want to point it over that way."

David tugs the switch and a trigger mechanism drops down. Even Ned is wide-eyed with astonishment. Drago rushes over.

"X! You get all the great toys. But I hopes better you shoots than scuba-dive."

David turns and ices Drago with an irritated look.

"Try a few rounds on the target, sir," Gilbert continues. "It's designed to be shot from the hip on the strap. Like this."

Gilbert helps David position the instrument for optimal balance.

"It's silenced, semi-auto, and packs quite a punch with an eight-round magazine of .300 Blackout." Gilbert points to the barely visible base-concealed magazine on the bottom edge of the guitar's body. David expertly pops it out, then snaps it back in.

"I'll try a stationary shot on the paper targets. Is it set up for close range?"

Gilbert nods.

"Got a great balance to it."

David faces the corridor and points the bass gun at two human-outline targets.

"X. Try to hit in head if you ca—"

Drago's sentence is cut short by a *chud-chud, chud-chud*. The sequence takes barely a second. Everyone looks downrange, but nothing has moved. Sophie walks to the side wall, presses a button, and the targets start reeling in on their chain mechanism.

Drago chuckles. "Idea is to shoots targets, not back wall!"

Sophie tears the sheets down and hands them to Drago.

"Oh..."

David has hit both targets for maximal lethality and effect- in the center of the face, with both rounds barely an inch apart in both groups.

"Some kids go to canoeing camp," David explains. "I went to shooting camp."

Ned looks guardedly proud, but Sophie can barely contain how impressed she is. David is a decent bassist, but when it comes to handling a firearm, he's a rock star.

"Fantastic, young man!" Gilbert says. "But now the pièce de résistance. If you flip this second switch, you now have a tranquilizer gun. No need to test it – and I'm afraid we don't have any suitable volunteers – but if you prefer the use of non-lethal force, this will do the trick."

"Definitely. How does it work?"

"Hit your target anywhere, ideally intramuscular," replies Gilbert. "The dart will instantly put your mark to sleep for five, maybe ten minutes. When they wake up, there will be a narcotic mixture coursing through their veins that should guarantee them the best New Year they ever had."

"That good, eh?"

"Quite so," Gilbert replies, convincingly enough that David wonders if he may have dabbled with some 'controlled testing' of the substance.

"That's it, then," McCarty says, checking his watch. "Gilbert will drive you to the mansion, where everything will be set up. Sophie will be there before midnight, and I will see you at the exfil site."

Drago puts his hand on David's shoulder.

"Okay, Mr. bigshot, time to puts toys away. I take to venue. I'm your road dog for tonight."

"That's roadie."

"Close enough," Drago replies.

Chapter 31
A Delusional Foe

A man of impeccable taste, Gilbert chauffeurs David to the show in a mint condition 1928 Cadillac. Coconut palms hang over the road, creating a kaleidoscopic tunnel of moving shadow and light as the car creeps along. A family of raccoons at roadside look up as the classic Capone vehicle thunders past, their eyes fluorescent-green in its headlights.

"When will Sophie be here?" David says, leaning forward from the back seat.

"Not to worry, sir. I'll have her at the venue before midnight."

"What about this double agent? How will I know if—"

"Ennio. Yes. Do keep your eyes open for anything strange," Gilbert interjects, "although, playing at a cult compound, the whole thing might seem a tad off."

"I hear that Huracan hates music."

"Oh, he despises it. His followers don't often hear music, so they may dance with depraved abandon."

"Just as long as everybody keeps their clothes on," David says, trying to inject some humor into the seriousness of what lies ahead.

"Well, they do practice some unusual sexual rituals," Gilbert replies.

"Oh dear."

"Ah. Here's the turnoff."

Gilbert wheels around a potholed corner, past Private Property and Keep Out signs. David looks through the windshield from the back as the car bumps down the rutted laneway.

"Why can't they take the missile out with an air strike? Or a commando raid? Surely that submarine out there could blast it to kingdom come."

Gilbert clarifies. "A whole lot of politics get involved when blowing up an atomic device on friendly soil. Plus, Huracan uses his followers as human shields. Combine that with millions in extortion and bribes, and no, we've explored the options. The best way is a good old-fashioned covert insertion. Once you modify the circuit, Ned will take control from that fancy boat of his, fly the damned thing out and detonate it over the open Atlantic."

"He's going to detonate a nuclear warhead?!"

"Oh, pray not, but do endeavor to install your circuit correctly." Gilbert stops in front of a chain-link security gate topped with razor wire. "You'll have to walk the rest of the way, my boy. The work permit is in your jacket pocket, just in case Immigration tries to spoil the party."

"Thanks, Gilbert. I'll let Sophie know if anything seems extra weird. Speaking of which—"

A solitary figure approaches the vehicle.

"Looks like Ganymede is here to escort you. Be careful of that one. He's got a violent criminal background."

"Why am I not surprised," David says. "Thank you, my good man, and a very Happy New Year to you. I look forward to sharing a stiff rum when this is all over."

"Indeed, sir. Make it two. Now do take good care of yourself and my precious Sophie."

"On my life," David assures Gilbert.

Ganymede arrives at David's door wearing pancake makeup and garish mascara with glittering eyelids. He's sporting red-and-yellow tuxedo tails over his congregation whites. The freakish disciple opens the rear door of the Caddy and greets David with a fake smile.

"Welcome to paradise, David. Not many outsiders are permitted on these hallowed grounds. I, for one, prefer it that way."

"Nice to see you too, Ganymede. Or is it Robin..."

"Oh, puh-lease. Your own fashion sense is truly yawn-inspiring."

"Got me there," David replies. He steps out of the car.

"We're beyond excited to hear your eighties set, so I shall now escort you to the Utopia Room."

A female security officer eyeballs them as they approach the gate, but Ganymede waves her off. They pass through the entranceway and follow a winding path dotted with footlights which leads to a splendid colonial building. A glorious wraparound porch is brimming with elegantly dressed partygoers, and the sound of a saxophone floats across the evening air. David notices that the patrons seem to be wearing wigs to cover their cropped hairdos.

"New Year's Eve here is like what you might call Halloween," Ganymede explains. "For one night a year, our lord permits us to dress as our previous selves. This reminds us of the futility of material life and the uselessness of the past. After midnight, we'll cast our clothes into a giant bonfire. Maybe even you will throw off your earthly possessions tonight, David."

"Don't think so," David says. "Not so sure about the Reverend's teachings. Especially this once-a-year music shit."

"The Great One is reconsidering his edict. You could join us, be our disciple of the arts."

David knows that organizations like this will say anything to woo people. He responds with an equal amount of bullshit.

"Really? I'll think about that!" he replies vigorously.

Ganymede appears puzzled by David's keen response as he leads him through a side doorway and up a set of stairs.

The party room's decor is typical New Year's chintz, with banners, balloons, noisemakers, and a mirrored disco ball. There are larger-than-life murals on the walls that portray Huracan as a deity. Onstage, a trio of musicians are playing soft jazz while a smattering of patrons dance like '70s acid trippers, but most of the guests are outside on the front porch. At the back of the ballroom, a small group of converts are seated cross-legged on the floor, chanting while a minder whaps them with a wooden ruler. At the far end of the dance floor, a roped-off platform and an empty throne await Huracan.

"I must leave you now, David. Will Sophie soon be joining us?"

"She'll be here."

"I shall attend to her personally."

Ganymede bows flamboyantly and leaves.

David ascends a set of stairs into the darkened wings, where his equipment is set up. Across the stage, a redhead in a paisley jacket motions at him from behind a stack of keyboards. She looks up from a Fender Rhodes piano as David walks over to her.

"Greetings. You must be David. I'm Stacey. I've printed out a set list, and there's a book of charts if you need them."

"Thanks, Stacey. You played here before?"

"A few times. It's always a bit 'out there', but hey—it's a gig. That's Bruce on drums and Tyrone on sax."

The musicians nod at David as they jam Miles Davis's All Blues.

"We're almost done the jazz tunes. We'll get into the eighties set twenty minutes from now. That'll take us up to midnight, and we'll be out of here before the grand speech."

"Sounds good. I'll check my gear and get tuned up."

David walks over to his keyboard at stage right. There's nobody around, so he opens its lid and raises the main circuit panel. He untucks the bottom of his shirt, then snaps the golden missile circuit board out of the keyboard. Stacey glances over, but her view is blocked by the keyboard's open lid, so David transfers the board into his waistband pocket. He reaches in and wriggles the second circuit board free, but the sound of approaching voices startles him. He rushes to secure the component, but his fingers stiffen and he drops it. The circuit bounces down the stairs into darkness.

"David Wesson?! What the fuck are you doing here?" a voice says.

David looks up and recognizes Chad Marshall, a guitarist from the Miami jobbing scene.

"Oh hey, Chad. Long time. I'm playing with you guys tonight."

Chad looks curiously at David's undone shirt hanging over his pants as a man with a pointy moustache emerges out of the darkness behind him and looks over Chad's shoulder. The mustachioed man is short and strong looking, dressed in a black suit, tight pants, with rose-tinted glasses. His head is topped with a porkpie hat.

Chad points at David's undone shirt.

"Looks like that's not all you're playing with, Wesson. Check it out, Reggie!"

The two of them giggle like schoolboy bullies. Quite frankly, Chad Marshall is someone David would prefer not to see. He's a spoiled fuckin' goof– one of those guys with a big mouth who doesn't pick up on normal social cues.

"Hey! Don't step on that chip," David says.

"Chips? Oh, man," Chad sighs. "I could go for some chips, eh, Reg? Oh, by the way, this is our singer, Reggie."

As Reggie shakes David's hand, something about him seems familiar, but David can't place it.

"You guys reek of pot," David says.

"So? It's a hell gig on New Year's Eve, man!" Chad leans over and whispers in David's ear. "By the way, ah, just let me know if you need a little bump." He points to his nose and makes a sniffing sound.

"Not a chance!" David replies. "Listen, I dropped something. Can you see it?"

"Is this what you're looking for?" a female voice replies.

Huracan's disciple Ariel steps out of the shadows, the circuit board between her thumb and forefinger. She stares icily at David.

"Why would you bring an old keyboard like that, Wesson?" Chad whines. He points at the vintage synth. "Those things are fuggin' ancient, right Reg!"

David's mind flashes to Sophie saying, 'In this business, one misstep, even one wrong expression, can get someone killed'. David searches for words as he tries to ignore Ariel's penetrating gaze

"They're finicky, but these Oberheims are amazing" he says, a bit too enthusiastically. "Perfect for 80s music. You'll see!".

Ariel's eyelids narrow. She hands over the computer chip and struts off.

When she exits the building, Ariel finds Ganymede standing outside the back door. He's huffing on a cigarette, fidgety and tense.

"I don't like that smart-ass," he whispers venomously. "And where's that little Sophie? After midnight, she is fucking done!" He clenches his teeth like a vicious animal.

"How are you going to do it?" Ariel asks.

Ganymede shrugs. "The bitch got drunk, fell off the pier and snapped her pretty little neck on the rocks. Hero boy dove in to save her and they found their bloated bodies the next day."

Ariel smiles and bows her head. "What a great honor our lord has tasked you with. If I can be of help, just wish it so," she says.

"I especially look forward to killing her," Ganymede replies, wiping a drop of saliva from his lower lip.

Chapter 32
Seven Minutes To Midnight

David has played many shows, but rarely has he witnessed such a fervent spectacle. It might have something to do with Huracan's denunciation of music, plus there's a rumor that half the patrons are high on magic mushrooms. That said, the band is tight, and David loves the feel of his custom bass. The dance floor is packed and the only person *not* having a good time is the Great Leader, who is hunched forward on his garish throne looking pouty, bored, and cranky, oblivious to the eruption of joy around him. From time-to-time Huracan covers his ears and glares at soundman Drago, who does his best to irritate the regal party-pooper by sneaking feedback into the mix.

David is impressed by singer Reggie's showmanship. His voice? Not so much. It's thin, strident, and almost every song is just out of his range. Plus, there's something about him that doesn't feel right, but David is probably over-analyzing. More importantly, he hasn't seen Sophie, and that is causing him deepening concern, especially since an enormous clock on the wall reads seven minutes to midnight.

The band segues from Rock Lobster into Burning Down the House, and the song is obviously Ganymede's favorite. He pogos like a spring-loaded puppet in his garish red-and-yellows. On every bounce his hands jitter like a man being electrocuted, and he mixes it up with the occasional slam-dance, taking out anyone who gets close to with a blindsiding bodycheck. In the far corner of the Utopia Room, the newbies are still being whapped about the head by their minder. David feels as if he's been transported into a painting by Hieronymus Bosch and wonders if he might have mistakenly ingested some psylocibin punch.

Halfway through the Nova-Sound Explosion's soul-rattling version of Burning Down The House, someone taps David's shoulder. He spins around and sees Sophie standing behind him. David is awestruck by her radiant elegance. He can't believe he's only known her for twenty-four hours. Emotionally, they've been through what some spend a lifetime trying to achieve. Then again, it's still possible that David *is* suffering from a severe case of Stockholm Syndrome.

Huracan couldn't care less about the party. He seems preoccupied with scattering his I Ching coins and scouring over their patterning, while Ariel stands deathly bored at his side. David guesses the leggy South

Asian beauty would prefer to be tumbling gymnastically to the beat rather than playing handmaiden to Huracan. With her tall and lean frame, she could easily be a dancer or martial arts champion, and she likely is both.

David starts rocking hard on his bass. He beams a smile on Ariel and refuses to avert. She eventually succumbs to his undeniable stage magnetism and glances back at him. David swears he sees a flicker of softness in her eye, before the pointed toe of a Manolo Blahnik bites into his calf. He winces and turns to see Sophie, her head cocked to the side, apparently unamused by his showbiz charm. David secretly loves that she's jealous.

He flips the bass over his back and struts up to his keyboard. Right on cue, he dives into the song's middle eight. Drago cranks David's riff out of the PA at a limb-rattling volume. The groove strengthens as everyone in the band picks up on his superb feel. Everyone, that is, except guitarist Chad, who suddenly looks pale and frightened. The shrooms are not mixing well with whatever the hell else he's on.

David starts feeling lost, in a good way, as the entourage begins playing synchronously like a single entity. He glances at Huracan, and sees the Reverend gazing down at his mystic coins. But as if sensing David's gaze, Huracan raises his head and locks a stare on him. Once again, David feels almost paralyzed by his soul-disturbing glare. Though the Reverend often acts like a petulant two-year-old, at core he is a charismatic criminal sociopath who wields immense power over people.

The entire congregation are now slam-dancing and pogoing in an increasingly violent manner. David can sense a shifting of the tide coming on. He no longer feels blissfully lost in the music, suddenly impacted by the gravitas of the approaching mission.

Reggie boogies up to David, doing a frantic James Brown dance. He grunts into the mic and points it at the audience. The audience grunts back. After repeating this call-and-answer shtick a couple more times, Reggie thrusts his hand out. He tosses the microphone at David.

"Catch!" he shouts.

As David snatches the mic, he is struck by the sight of Reggie's crazed-looking eyes. The singer's voice and even his throwing motion have a familiarity to them. David also notices that the left side of Reggie's moustache is lower than the right.

A shiver races from the base of David's spine to the hairs on the back of his neck. "Reggie" is the goateed client who came to his house for the synthesizer repair. He's also the drunk vagrant who harassed David while Sophie swapped bags at the bus stop. But most damning of all, he recognizes Reggie as the wild-eyed assassin from the Greater God church who shot Aaden, then threw the smoking gun at David and fingered him for murder.

David tosses the mic back to the cheeseball singer, who catches it then continues his showy routine by duck-walking across the stage. David resumes playing his bass guitar. He grooves over to Sophie and tries to convey his discovery to her, but it's impossible to communicate since Drago has pushed the PA to a near sonic explosion. Plus, Bruce is channeling his inner Fleetwood in an extended drum solo.

"Ennio is here!" David shouts at Sophie.

"What?"

"The singer... is the rogue agent."

"Can't hear you."

"The singer is—" David tips his head toward Reggie, who's at front stage convulsing like a rooster on meth.

"Ennio. The double agent."

Sophie's expression flattens. She points to David, then to herself. Sophie holds up five fingers and motions toward the back exit. David understands. In five minutes, they will be out of here.

Just then, a crash erupts from the far end of the room. The crowd lets out a collective gasp. They turn and see Huracan standing atop his velvet-roped stage, fists shaking. An upside-down table lies beside a shattered vase and smashed tea set on the floor in front of him. The veins in the

Reverend's forehead look as if they're about to pop.

"Enough of this drivel!" he screams.

Ariel steps in front of him and motions with her long, thin arms for everyone to *back off*. Ganymede looks back and spots Huracan's rage. A cruel grin stretches across the disciple's face and he storms the stage. Ganymede climbs up onto it with fists swinging and clocks Chad right in the kisser. The dopey guitarist teeters and crashes to the floor.

Another young man climbs up and charges Stacey. She backs away in time to see her beloved keyboard stack fall. Bruce concludes his solo, then climbs over his kit and starts pounding the assailant's head with a mallet. The PA starts squealing with feedback, angering Huracan even more. Then, the wigs come off, clothes start flying, and in seconds the entire congregation has morphed into an angry mob of white jumpsuits and angular hairdos.

David unplugs his bass. He steps in front of Sophie as a cult member rushes her in a screaming banzai charge. David flips the hidden switch and the bass gun's trigger drops into position. Just as a collision seems imminent, David snaps his instrument forward. The blunt end of the neck strikes the man between the eyes with such cringeworthy force that the strings rattle. The attacker drops like a rag doll.

"Follow me!" Sophie shouts.

David backs toward her, sweeping his bass-gun in front of him, ready to lay down fire. They scramble down the stairs and out the back door, then bolt for the darkness of the woods. Sophie stops to get her bearings while David watches their back, but no one seems to be following them.

"This way," she whispers loudly.

As they stumble through the moonlit forest over rocks and through a tangled patch of love vine, the cacophony of sound gradually fades into the distance. Sophie stops in front of a massive moss-covered bunker. David doubles over, almost retching from the intense physical effort.

Coming from the direction of the Utopia Room, they hear a tinny, 1920s brass quintet version of Auld Lang Syne. The obligatory anthem is short-lived, however. It screeches to a stop that is followed by the crash of its record player being smashed. Then, the distorted, ranting voice of Huracan.

David glances at Sophie as she catches her breath.

"Happy New Year."

Chapter 33
Bliss And Fear

Standing in front of the concrete bunker, David notices pipes protruding from the ground. Beneath them, a rumbling sound. Sophie switches a red-lensed flashlight on and motions for David to follow her. After pushing through some scrubby vegetation, they arrive at a clearing on the far side of the imposing structure. David watches as Sophie begins kicking the ground with the toe of her shoe. One of her kicks produces a hollow sound. She leans down and starts clearing brush from the forest floor. A thick, rectangular piece of wood appears, the lid to a sturdy wooden crate. David swings the bass off his back and leans it against the bunker.

"Pirate treasure?" he asks.

"Supplies. Courtesy of Mr. Pong. Pirate treasure would be the ten million in gold that Huracan has buried here somewhere."

"Count me in."

They pry the crate open and Sophie starts unpacking it. She hands David a submachine pistol and a second firearm.

"A suppressed MPK and a sawed-off Remington," he says. "Impressive. Pong knows his up-close-and-personal."

"Actually, these are from my collection," Sophie clarifies. "Hopefully we won't have to use them." She passes David a heavy bag containing an orange hazmat coverall. At the back of the bag he sees a helmet and breathing apparatus.

"Jacket and tie in the bag, hazmat suit over the rest of your clothes. You've got the circuits, right?"

"Roger that, but I couldn't get to the tool kit during ballroom blitz."

"You won't need it here. I've got an extra one for the briefcase."

David hands the machine pistol back to Sophie. She attaches a strap to the MPK and slings it over her shoulder. David removes his jacket while Sophie retrieves an extended ammo magazine from the crate. It makes a clacking sound as she snaps it in.

"Actually, can I borrow your jacket?" she asks.

He passes it to her and she drapes it over her bare shoulders and chiffon dress.

David smiles. "Girl, you have no idea how cute you look in Armani."

"Knock it off, David! They're probably out looking for us, and the Rev's yacht is barely a hundred feet away, so keep it down."

"Sorry. I always dumb up when I'm nervous. Have you got the boots?"

Sophie rummages through the crate. "Damn. I don't see them."

"Good thing I didn't wear white socks, then." Sophie looks over and sees that David's hazmat suit legs are an inch short, drawing attention to his Bruno Magli dress shoes. For the first time, Sophie seems unsure.

"I wish I could laugh right now," she says. "I just want this to be over."

"Hey, it's going to be fine," David assures her. "We'll celebrate tomorrow. New Year's Day. Come to think of it, it's my birthday tomorrow."

"That's right!" Sophie exclaims. "I remember that from your file. But it's already after midnight, so that means it's your birthday right now. Don't tell me. Thirty-two?"

"Close. Thirty-three. I hope you don't mind being with an older man who hasn't made his first million."

"You're not *that* much older than me," she digs. "What do you want for your birthday?"

"To tell you the truth, I haven't even thought about it," David says, then he becomes uncharacteristically shy. "I don't know," he mumbles. "Maybe if we get back to Miami tomorrow, and you're not doing anything. I mean... you probably have plans and all, but, maybe you could come over."

Sophie stares into David's eyes but reveals nothing.

"We could order Chinese, lie in bed and watch Humphrey Bogart movies all day drinking red wine. I think I've even got some of that popcorn you cook on the stove. Then again, I can't see as rare a diamond as you being—"

Sophie flips her hand up, silencing David mid-sentence. She draws the machine pistol out from under her jacket and crouches into a combat stance. She motions for David to fall in behind her. As he does so, he hears a strange, steel-on-stone scraping sound from around the corner. It's as if a heavy door is being opened. Then, a patter of feet on leaves, a stick cracking. Sophie flips the MPK's safety off. David eyes the pump-action shotgun behind him. Sophie switches her gun barrel flashlight on and it spotlights a haggard looking man emerging from the brush. The man shields his eyes as he stumbles toward them.

"Stop!" Sophie commands, but the man continues forward. He's weak, staggering, wearing an orange hazmat suit.

"Who are you?" Sophie barks.

"I'm not one of them. I swear," the man says, almost crying. "Please. Get me out of here."

Sophie cocks her weapon. "What's your name?"

"Stonewall. Professor Christian Stonewall."

"What's the code word and countersign, Professor?"

Tears start forming in the man's eyes. He seems to be on the edge of a nervous breakdown.

"I can't remember," he sobs. "I barely remember my own name. Please. We need water. Everyone's dying down there."

David charges over and steadies the desperate man.

"Hey, it's okay. We're friends," David says. "Here now, you're burning up."

He unzips Stonewall's suit and leads him to a stump, where the professor collapses into a seated position with his head hung low. Sophie rushes to the supply crate. She pulls out a water bottle and a small square bundle. She hurries back and passes the bottle to Stonewall, who chugs furiously from it.

"Not too fast or it'll make you sick, Professor."

"You have to find my son," he begs. "I shouldn't be here with you. They'll kill me. They'll kill us all."

"You're safe with us," David assures the broken man.

Sophie passes the professor a paper-wrapped square. "Do you like chocolate?"

Stonewall snatches it from her and gnaws off a corner. His mood instantly lightens. "Oh. That is so good. I can't remember the last time we had anything to eat."

"It will energize you and calm your nerves. Now take a moment and settle."

Stonewall's demeanor eases momentarily, but he becomes delirious again. "Don't make me go back in there. You have no idea what these monsters are capable of."

"Hey, buddy. You're in the home stretch," David assures the broken man. "I'm coming in with you. You just show me where, and I'll do the rest. Okay?"

"Do you have the circuit?" Stonewall asks as Sophie returns to the crate and removes a small, cylindrical red tin.

She peels off its vacuum-packed top, then passes the tin to the professor.

"Pringles chips? There is a god," he says.

Stonewall crunches a mouthful and washes the crumbs down with water. He follows with a bite of chocolate and repeats.

"I have the circuits in my waist pouch," David says.

"Good. There's not much time. Security went to the main lodge, but they'll be back soon. If that rocket isn't upright and being fueled in an hour, people are going to start getting hurt."

David turns toward Sophie. "Do you have a sidearm I can take?" he asks discreetly.

Sophie reaches into the crate and retrieves a Smith & Wesson 745.

"No!" Stonewall interjects. "There's fuel vapor down there. One spark and this entire bay will go up in a giant fireball."

"What about a tranquilizer pistol that uses a CO2 cartridge?" Sophie asks.

The professor nods as he savors his last morsel of chocolate.

Sophie passes the dart pistol to David, who stuffs it into his hazmat pocket and helps the professor to his feet.

"When we get onsite," Stonewall states in a more commanding tone, "first of all, no talking. Understand? None."

David nods.

"Secondly, at all cost, avoid contact with the two security officers, Audrius and Brutus. Thirdly, we need to exchange the circuitry as quickly as possible. I cannot stress that enough. I will do my best to get you out, but worst-case, you'll be stuck in there with the rest of us until they release us. If they release us."

"Don't worry, professor," Sophie assures him. "Everyone is getting out tonight, including you and your boy."

He reaches over and squeezes Sophie's hand.

"Bless you, child," Stonewall says. He turns toward David. "Come with me, son. I hope you're not afraid of heights."

"Heights?"

He leads David around a corner toward a six-inch-thick open door. It looks like a relic from a submarine, with a steel locking wheel on the inside of it and metal flanges spaced evenly at its edges.

"Put your respirator on, and watch your step," the professor advises.

David pokes his head through the doorway. He shudders as he looks down a rickety ladder that vanishes into a concrete hole four stories deep. The air is thick and toxic.

"What about ... radiation?" David asks, choking on his words.

"The warhead is secure, so radioactivity is nominal. But the fumes are bad, so wear your goggles and breather. Before we enter the rocket chamber, you'll need to put your helmet on. Now come. We must go. After you."

David takes a shaky breath and prepares to swing his foot over the top rung of the ladder.

"Hold up!" Sophie commands. "One more thing."

She walks up to David.

"Butter or margarine?"

He looks at her, confused.

"For the popcorn."

"Why butter, of course," David scoffs.

"Good. Then tomorrow we celebrate. For god's sake be careful, and I will meet up with you real soon. Okay? I promise." Sophie stands on her tiptoes and kisses David on the cheek. He feels his heart gushing from a strange mixture of bliss and fear.

Chapter 34
A Liturgy Of Lies

Flanked by his highest-ranking disciples, the Reverend addresses the congregation. His followers, all in uniform whites now, crowd the stage and look up in awe at their leader. Huracan steadies himself with a ceremonial mace. Around his neck is an ornamental jade chain, at the end of which dangles a totemistic Mayan head.

"Tonight, we return to the beginning! Where history shall be decreed in only *my* name. Your immaculate Lord Huracan spawned humanity, then with great displeasure he washed it away with a great flood. Tonight, I wash the galaxy of the unworthy once again!"

The crowd responds with frenzied adulation, but Ariel raises a finger to her soft lips and the room silences. The Reverend continues, his voice soft, hypnotic.

"The world you *think* you know exists because I will it so. And you exist because I *dream* you so." His voice crescendos: "Your entire so-called universe is a single neuron firing in my mind—a mind ten trillion times that of a feeble human mind."

The crowd are dumbstruck, even offended, but Ganymede leads them into applause.

"Only my truest followers shall prevail once the world is re-ordained in my name. Huracan's name!"

"Thank you Great Lord!" the congregation cries out in unison.

"Tonight, my most worthy shall become a god. A lesser god than I, yes, but every ... single ... one of you shall possess the power of ten thousand meagre humans! And for this privilege, this precious gift, I, the great Huracan, permit you to worship me!"

The followers fall to their knees and begin chanting as Ganymede pumps his fist in the air: " Hur-a-can... Hur-a-can..."

Huracan hands Ganymede the microphone.

"The new devotees shall now come forward to be indoctrinated," he announces.

The wooden sticked handler leads the converts to the front of the stage, where they form a line and fall to bended knee. Ganymede descends from the stage and walks past them, conducting an inspection. He stops at the line's center and looks down at an elderly man knelt before him. Ganymede smiles lovingly, then wrenches the man's head forward by the ears and knees him full force in the chest. The man drops to the floor and the disciple starts kicking him in the abdomen. The congregation roars. Everyone rushes the new recruits and starts beating them in a violent hazing ritual. Huracan beckons at Ariel, who hurries to his side.

"When Ganymede is finished the purification, tell him I need," he mumbles, pointing to the IV stent in the crook of his elbow.

"Ganymede shall soon attend to you, lord," Ariel assures the Reverend.

"Where is the girl and her man?" he asks through dry, pursed lips.

"Shall I find them, greatness?"

"Locate them and bring them to me. Dead or alive, it does not matter. The countdown will soon commence. No one shall stand in my way.

Two-thirds of the way down the artesian structure, thirty feet below the surface, David finds it best to focus on one rung at a time. Every muscle is aching, and it's so hot inside his hazmat suit, it feels like he's wearing a sauna. Entire sections of the ladder creak and sway from missing wall bolts as David and Professor Stonewall descend into darkness.

"Almost there, lad. You okay?" Stonewall wheezes, his voice enveloped in an unearthly echo inside the vertical space.

"I'm fine, professor. What happens next?"

"If you look down, carefully, you'll see a reddish glow. That's the floor and the end of the ladder. But the last rung is loose and the ground uneven, so go easy. Once you step off, stay where you are. Perhaps you can steady me when I get there."

"Got it. How far to the rocket?"

"Just beyond the north wall, there's an L-shaped room with a hidden opening into the chamber. But we need to get there quickly, before security returns. Apparently there was some sort of kerfuffle at the New Year's bash."

"Ah, yes. A kerfuffle. Okay, I'm at the loose rung and ... down."

David steps onto the pitted floor, but the screech of human flesh on steel makes him shudder. He looks up and sees the professor sliding out of control. David lunges forward to catch him, but Stonewall lands hard.

"My ankle!" Stonewall limps to keep the weight off his right foot, which has rolled over on its side. "I don't think it's broken, but god that hurts."

"Can you put any pressure on it?" David asks, guilty of losing focus. "That's it. Walk it off."

"I'll be fine," Stonewall says, panting and struggling on the misaligned joint. "We've got to keep moving."

David locks his arm around him, and they navigate through the dark alcove. The professor is gradually able to put weight back on his foot, and they soon arrive at the hidden opening to the missile chamber.

"I'll go in first, then signal for you to come through," Stonewall whispers. "There are technicians in there and they will notice you, but believe me, not one of them will say a word. The poor buggers are too damn scared. Now remember, no eye contact with security, and hopefully that sadist Ganymede doesn't show up. I will guide you to the missile, then assist while you swap out the circuit. Take it out of your pouch now and put it in your left pocket. Good luck, my friend, and thank you."

David feels his pulse quickening as he removes the circuit board from his waistband. He stuffs it into his hazmat pocket while the professor squeezes through the opening. After receiving the professor's hand signal, David dons his helmet and crawls on through.

Unlike the dazzling clean rooms of NASA, Huracan's subterranean missile chamber is a filthy dungeon. Mesh-caged spotlights surge and flicker, water oozes from mossy walls, and an electrifying hum seems to surround them. Down the center of the chamber, the olive-drab colored rocket is laid out on a pair of rusted steel rails. At its bottom there is a hydraulic hinging mechanism, clearly for raising the weapon into launch position.

The lower section houses a vectored rocket engine which, after years of reading his father's Aviation Week magazines, David recognizes is of extremely advanced design.

A shorter middle area contains the guidance section, and at the rocket's top, the menacing nuclear payload lies separated from its body like a decapitated head. Three technicians are busy securing a nose cone over the warhead, and a fourth is curled lifelessly in a fetal position on the floor. David tries not to dwell on the presence of the motionless body, but it quickly becomes clear that the technicians here are expendable. He follows Stonewall across a loud metal catwalk to the guidance module. There, the professor targets a lamp at the rocket's inner workings. David leans in for a closer look and is relieved to discover that the circuit looks identical to the one in his pocket.

Stonewall passes him a hexagonal tool and David uses it to twist four pins that hold the circuit board in place. He disconnects two connectors by carefully wiggling them apart. David glances up to take a calming breath and sees that the technicians are staring at him through their fogged-up visors. The two men and a woman look emaciated and exhausted, but more than anything, they look frightened. David reassures them with an "okay" signal, and the technicians return to sliding the nose cone over the obsidian-black warhead.

Stonewall reaches into the guidance module and removes the circuit panel while David slides the SV-335 circuit board out of his pocket. Fearful of dropping it, he maneuvers it over the pins quickly. The professor's eyes widen when he sees the gold-laden component glinting. But just as an excited smile seems to develop around the corners of his eyes, a brash metallic clatter shatters their focus. The chamber's steel door starts ratcheting upward.

Audrius, Huracan's machine-gun-toting henchman swaggers through the entranceway, wearing khaki pants, a gray suit jacket, goggles and a respirator. The door thunders shut behind him. David lowers his gaze as Stonewall motions frantically for him to hurry.

David pushes on the circuit board. It clicks into place. Using the hexagonal wrench, he gives each of the pins a half twist clockwise. His heart feels as if it is going to burst through his chest as Audrius sways toward them, looking wider with every step. David secures the first connector and weaves the second cable into position as Huracan's enforcer looms.

Barely six feet away from them, Audrius flips his gun up. He starts shoving the professor, yelling at him in what sounds like Russian. Stonewall tries to explain that the rocket is almost ready, but Audrius backhands him across the face. Stonewall crumples to the floor. It is everything David can do to not intervene. He hurries to finalize the circuit, but suddenly, there's a problem: the second connector doesn't fit.

There has been a vital communication breakdown. Without that crucial intersect, the missile will likely lift off, then fall on its side and explode, incinerating everything within a half-mile radius. Worse, in the event of such a failure, a suicidal Huracan might detonate the doomsday machine. A nuclear explosion would transform this island paradise into a hundred-mile-wide, 20,000-year-long radioactive wasteland.

What to do, what to do?

Audrius smiles. He raises his gun and prepares to beat the life out of the professor. As David wonders how on earth he can stop the security goon, a flash of insight strikes like a thunderbolt. He takes a deep breath, gathers every micron of his will and faces the two men. Then, in the best faux-German accent he can muster David shouts:

"Was ist das?!"

Audrius slowly turns and faces David, who suddenly feels nauseous—from the fear, the heat, the stale air, the exhaustion, the pressure of the last forty hours, the slave-like conditions here, the monstrous weapon in front of him and the so-called deity who controls these people with a liturgy of lies. But strangely, at this pivotal moment, David can think only of one thing: Sophie Bisset. What has become of her? God forbid she's been captured. Perhaps Ganymede has her and is torturing her for information. David owes her his life– and he promised Gilbert that he would protect "my precious Sophie."

Thoughts of Sophie only strengthen David's resolve. He straightens his posture and puffs his chest out, the way a wild animal makes itself look bigger when cornered. For the first time in his life, David Wesson is ready to kill if forced to do so. He walks robotically toward Audrius and stops between him and Professor Stonewall, who is at his feet. The barrel-chested henchman glares at David with lifeless eyes, but David is undeterred. He thrusts his hand out, stopping inches away from Audrius's chest. David channels his fury into a voice that bellows out of his throat like a bullet exiting the barrel of a gun.

"Halt!" he commands.

Chapter 35
Histrionics

David takes an enormous risk with such histrionics, but what's done is done. He's able to speak conversational German after spending a number of his teen years near Frankfurt, West Germany, when his father was stationed at Wiesbaden. Of course, if Audrius is local to that area, Wesson will have slipped a noose over his own neck. His patchy dialect will betray him and the ruse will be up. But the deception seems to have worked and the gunman eases, as much as a soulless killer can.

David grabs Stonewall's arm. He points hastily at the rocket and grunts loudly in short phrases, pretending to speak broken English.

"Das rauket. Get. Up. Schnell!"

Audrius seems puzzled, but yields to David's posturing. The gunman prods at Stonewall, toying with him like a cat playing with an injured mouse as David helps the professor to his feet.

"Das iz gut," David assures the stone-faced security man. "Danke shön."

David leads Stonewall to the missile and points at the connector that won't fit. The professor nods wearily. He limps to a tool cabinet, opens a drawer and returns with a six-to-five pin adapter. David snaps the connector into place and secures the wires. Stonewall tests the circuit with a pair of metal probes, and after receiving a series of green lights on a meter, the technicians begin to seam the sections together. Audrius looks off with disinterest as David uses a pneumatic socket wrench to tighten bolts near the engine housing. The female technician attaches a series of external cables and hoses for fueling and pre-launch power. In under an hour, the needle-shaped harbinger of destruction is together in one piece.

David fights off an unshakable feeling of guilt when he looks down at the missile that is six times his height. After all, he has helped to assemble a vessel capable of unfathomable destruction. Hopefully everything will go as planned, but that seems anything but likely. Judging by the hellish conditions in this wretched chamber, he'll be amazed if the damned thing even fires up.

The professor stands away from the rocket and each of the technicians respond by stepping away from the obelisk and placing their hands behind their back. David mimics them and falls in line. Stonewall retrieves a moss-green walkie-talkie.

"Commence lifting phase. I repeat: Commence lifting phase."

An overhead emergency beacon starts painting the room with a circulating red wash, as heavy servo motors pound into action with a pulsating murmur. With a groan, the track starts angling toward a concrete ceiling four stories above their heads. It's hard to believe that the missile will even fit within the confines of the bunker. It's going to be tight.

David fights off a sudden tinge of homesickness and nausea, but his plight, so far at least, is nothing compared with that of the souls imprisoned in this purgatory. He fears for their well-being as he does for his own. And David still has no idea how, or even if he will be extricated. He desperately needs to complete the last part of his duty: the exchange of circuitry in Huracan's control briefcase.

A brash metallic sound signals the sectional door rolling upward again. As it rises, a slender female form is revealed. Huracan's left-winger Ariel is standing in the opening, silhouetted by the starkly lit hallway behind her. She is now dressed in the congregation's regulation jumpsuit, although a lengthy non-regulation ponytail hangs over her shoulder. At her waist, a holstered sidearm. *Is this the part where we get lined up and shot?* David wonders. He can tell that others are thinking the same thing. At least one of the technicians is crying.

Ariel enters the chamber. She walks over to Audrius and whispers in his ear. Audrius instantly spins and locks his gun on David, who raises his hands, all the while thinking about the tranquilizer pistol in his pocket.

"Professor!" Ariel barks, without taking her eyes off David. "When will fueling begin?"

"Within the hour, mistress. The rocket must be completely upright."

"No more holdups, professor! Understand?"

"Of course not, mistress."

Ariel unholsters a World War II Luger with a silencer attached to it—a murderous weapon if there ever was one. David can tell by the way she handles it that Ariel is no stranger to firearms.

"You. Come with me," she commands, wagging the barrel at him. David saunters toward her, his hands above his head. Ariel motions at the doorway and he shuffles past her into the tunnel. She targets the pistol at the middle of his back as the door rattles shut behind them.

Topside, behind the concrete bunker, Sophie checks her watch. The last two hours have been excruciating. Partiers have been reveling in the woods and patrols are still roaming close by. David should have been up and out by now. Plus, they need to get to Huracan's control device immediately. The munitions crate has been closed and re-covered, but Sophie has kept a few guns hidden in the surrounding vegetation. She's changed out of her party dress into something more op-suitable: camo tights, army boots, with a tunic and leather holster around her waist.

The quiet is interrupted by the unmistakable sound of a pump-action shotgun being racked.

"Well, well," a voice says in a sickly sweet tone, before it sours. "Hands in the air."

Sophie follows the order implicitly. She hears footsteps approaching across the forest floor. A hand grabs her and spins her around. Ganymede is standing barely a foot away, so close that she can smell the reek of alcohol on his breath. His hair is sticking out every which way like a ball of wire and the pupils of his eyes look like saucers. He twitches and foams at the corners of his mouth as he looks Sophie up and down.

"My my. You and I are going to have such a good time," he says.

He reaches for her top button, but she twists away. Sophie feels an explosion of pain as Ganymede's elbow drives into the softness of her left temple. She feels herself falling, unable to raise her arms to cushion the landing. She hits the ground face-first and rolls onto her back, gasping for air. Ganymede looks down at her, seething like a rabid dog. He crunches his boot into her arm, twists his foot, and Sophie cries out as its tread tears into her bicep. The psychotic minion looks up at the stars, hands shaking. He lets out a high-pitched laugh that dissolves into a scream.

"Bitch!"

Chapter 36
Dire Complications

"Yes, sir. Of course, sir. No, not yet. Still waiting for phase one confirmation. Should be any time soo—"

Ned McCarty yanks the red telephone away from his head in an attempt to save his right eardrum. The phone's speaker explodes with a barrage of expletives and words such as F-18, the President, and submarine.

"There'd be casualties, General. Fifty to a hundred, plus 'Ruthie and her friends.'" McCarty brings the phone back to his ear. "Of course not, sir. Not compared to a nuclear expl—" His eyes dart nervously. "Two and a half hours?" Worry clouds Ned's face. "Yes, General Passmore, I understand. Two hours. Very good, sir. Confidence is high. Will keep you apprised."

Ned hangs up the phone.

"Asshole!"

He takes a calming sip of tea, then ascends a steep set of stairs.

The stars above glint like pinholes of light poking through a black velvet dome. A wispy crescent moon wobbles from side to side as if hanging from a pin, an effect created by the offshore waves lifting and releasing the Lady Argon at anchor. Ned shakes off a head of steam into the cool ocean air as he makes his way across the deck. Crewman Collins knows better than to ask as he peers through binoculars across the moonlit wavetops at the Greater God compound, two and a half miles away.

"Okay. Let's try this again," McCarty says, although he might as well be talking to himself. He picks up a rectangular control device and extends a collapsible antenna from its top center. The upper section has three banks of six switches. Below the switches at the left, middle, and right positions, are three toggles. Beneath these are three brightly colored buttons: yellow, green and blue, and on the lower right a red knob is covered by a safety latch with a skull-and-crossbones emblem above it.

Ned references some notes on a clipboard and turns a key while checking a multitude of tiny dip switches. At the top of the control box, a red LED starts blinking. Its pulse starts increasing in frequency, then with a loud beep it switches to a solid green color. McCarty clenches his hand into a fist.

"Yes! The rocket's guidance board is responding."

"Congratulations, sir. Any update on an air strike?" Collins grumbles.

"Let's just say that Bird One better be out of her nest within the next two hours, or the Breakwater Estate is going to look like the surface of the moon."

Back in the underground, David Wesson struggles to formulate a plan. He hasn't contacted anyone on the team in hours, and the slightest misstep could lead to a bullet in the back of his neck. But fortunately, even if for this brief moment, David Wesson is beyond fear.

"Interesting choice of shoes," Ariel remarks as she marches him up the dank corridor.

David sighs. He'd forgotten about his short-legged pants and designer shoes. He decides to stay with the success of his German routine.

"Sprechen du Deutsch?" he asks, his voice muffled through the helmet's visor.

"You mean 'Sprichst Sie Deutsch?'" Ariel replies. "Yes, I do speak German, and you obviously don't. Now helmet off. Nice and slow."

It feels heavenly getting the headpiece off, but there is a choking waft of chemical vapor in the air.

"Now turn around, David Wesson."

Cover blown. Mission over.

"Got me there," David says, as if he's been caught playing some childish game.

"How stupid do you think we are?" Ariel taunts. "You guys are a joke. Now off with the hazmat suit, no funny stuff. I'm quite handy with a Luger."

"I'll do exactly as you say," he replies.

He avoids using words like *relax* or *calm down*. Based on past marital misadventures, he knows that such words rarely go over well. But Wesson has a plan, albeit a bold one. While grasping the helmet with his left hand, he unzips the suit with his right. When he reaches its midsection, he clutches the rubbery material until he can feel the tranquilizer pistol in its pocket. While peeling the suit downward, he squeezes the pistol up and out. David drops the helmet and it bounces across the concrete floor. With Ariel momentarily distracted, Wesson palms the pistol and stuffs it into his pant pocket. The diversion seems to have worked.

"Push the suit to the side with your foot. And keep your hands where I can see them," the frigid disciple orders. "There's a door up ahead. Walk toward it."

David approaches the barred doorway. Behind it, women and men are cowering, begging for water. There's a horrible stench coming out of what looks like a darkened cave.

"Stop!" Ariel commands. "Take the key."

"You're going to put me in there? You do understand that when your 'great leader' lights up the rocket, this entire area will be incinerated."

"Silence!" Ariel barks. She throws the key to David as more worn-out souls arrive at the doorway, their clothes filthy and torn.

David opens the lock. As he starts prying on the door to open it, Ariel makes an announcement.

"This is your lucky night, people," she says. "You have served your lord well. Now out with you all. Proceed to section thirteen on the north side. There you'll find water, food and medical supplies. Under no circumstances are you to leave that location. Understood?"

Some of the slaves are so weak they can barely stand. A parade of skeletal bodies with sunken eyes exits the filthy prison cell.

"Thank you, Mistress Ariel," and "Huracan be praised," David hears them saying in dry, choked voices. He is disgusted. Huracan's paradise is nothing more than a concentration camp.

"What happens now?" he asks, barely able to suppress his fury.

"You and I are going to meet up with your little girlfriend."

"Sophie?! What have you done with her?" David rages.

"What have I done?" Ariel replies, almost laughing. "Oh, you don't have to worry about me. But God help her if brother Ganymede is there ahead of us. So, if you think you can keep your big-boy pants on, we're going to go find her. Understand? And don't even *think* of getting all heroic!"

216

They shuffle up the dank and crumbling corridor toward Huracan's private elevator. Ariel punches a series of numbers into a panel and the door swishes open.

"Hands behind your head. Step in and face the corner."

"It's not too late for you, Ariel," David says, trying to reason with the sultry brown-eyed disciple as he walks into the elevator. "An international court will be far more lenient if you stop this madness right now."

"No more talk, Wesson. I've had a long day," Ariel replies as the door rumbles shut behind her.

David couldn't agree more. He's exhausted and running dangerously low on bravado. It's time to just play along. Besides, he's got no other move. They ride the lift up and exit into the leader's opulent suite, but there's no Sophie, no anyone. It occurs to David that the scene is uncomfortably reminiscent of Tommy "getting made" in Goodfellas.

"Where is she!"

"Don't get all angry at me, Wesson! This is your game. Calm. Down."

Ariel is one sassy diva, he thinks.

As they walk across Huracan's elegant suite, he can't resist an eye roll and cringe as they pass the multi-person circular bed. Ariel orders him to sit behind an antique Louis XIV desk, then she holds out her hand.

"Now let's have the tranq gun."

David is both busted and beyond theatrics. He pulls the CO2 pistol from his pocket and drops it on the desk. His head falls back, a boxer between rounds. Ariel snatches the gun and swaggers toward a bookcase at the far side of the room. Then curiously, she makes a series of coded knocks on the shelf's side panel. A four-foot-wide section of the bookcase swings open, revealing a portal to a hidden room. David watches in amazement as Ariel, now strangely catlike and seductive, unzips the front of her jumpsuit to just below her cleavage and stretches her arms out lovingly. With a smile and a wiggle, she disappears from view into the chamber.

"Bru-tus! Happy New Year, baby. Gimme a kiss," David hears her say. Ariel's sweetness is followed by a *fwapp*, then a *thrrump* that sounds like a sack of potatoes hitting the floor.

A moment later, Ariel walks out of the room toward David. She nonchalantly drops the tranquilizer pistol on the desk, then surprisingly, the Luger.

"Go," she says, fluttering her hand toward the bookcase door. "I thought you wanted to play football."

"Football?" Wesson puzzles for a moment, then leaps out of his chair. "The control device!"

Ariel flips him off. She walks into the suite's kitchen, where she opens a fridge door.

"Beer?"

David charges into the secret chamber, barely noticing Brutus the wonder thug unconscious on the floor. Behind the henchman, atop a desk amid a roomful of mechanical dials and equipment, is Huracan's nuclear football, launch control for Bird One.

Chapter 37
Scorned

David lays the control case on top of the desk. He has no idea what to do with it now. He knows the case is booby-trapped, and only Sophie has the tools to open it. David struggles to stay focused as Bollywood-diva Ariel sashays over and plops a frosty can in front of him. Water droplets bead on the silvery, odd-shaped cylinder.

"I trust you won't spill this," she says. "We don't need any accidental launches."

"I have no idea how to open it," David admits.

"What?! This is the sloppiest operation I've ever seen! I knew you'd screw this up, Wesson."

David can't believe how much Ariel reminds him of his ex-wife.

"In the desk," she hisses, then, "You're welcome."

He opens the bottom desk drawer and finds a tool kit there.

What a drama queen she is, David thinks, although he can't deny her highbrow charisma. Ariel prances to the fridge like a gazelle and retrieves a bottle of rosé as David takes a chug of Sapporo.

"God, that is good," he says, glancing up at her. "So how long have you been on our side?"

"Whoa! No questions! Did they not teach you that on day one?"

"Actually, this *is* day one," David snipes.

Ariel's expression flattens. "Lord help us all."

She pours herself a slender glassful and waves her hand for David to move out of the way. Ariel leans in and starts opening the device with the focus of a Swiss watchmaker.

"If you do it in the wrong order," she explains, "you'll release phosgene gas."

"Phosgene? Nasty stuff," he replies. World War I chemical warfare. One whiff and—"

"Could you shut up and shed some light over here?"

David points a wire-thin halogen lamp beam onto the briefcase. Ariels pull out a ring of keys with a tiny three-pronged tool on it. She inserts it into a receptacle at the bottom of the case, gives it a twist, then loosens two hidden fittings. The lid pops open, revealing a brushed-aluminum faceplate punctuated by a trio of yellow, green and red buttons with key slots on either side of them. Near the bottom of the device, there is a numeric keypad, which David assumes is to enter launch codes. Ariel pushes a hexagonal metal rod into a barely visible hole. Upon hearing a click, she rotates it to the left and the unit's face panel springs up, unmasking a tangle of wires and circuitry. Ariel points a slender finger at her chest.

"I'm the best," she self-congratulates, before taking an elegant sip of rosé. The pale-pink elixir barely touches her lips.

"Will Sophie be meeting us here?" David asks. "I hope she's okay."

Ariel chokes. "Emotional involvement? You really need to get back to spy school, Wesson. If you're still alive after all this, that is. You are expendable, in case she forgot to tell you that part. Juicy assignment, though. You must be good at s—"

Ariel is cut short by the sound of keys rattling at the suite's exterior door. She snatches the Luger and lowers her voice. She looks at David, suddenly deadly serious.

"Stay where you are. And don't mess this up."

She looks past David and with just a touch more volume than necessary, shouts, "Hands in the air, Wesson."

Ariel backs away, her gun aimed at David's head. The outside door bursts open and Sophie stumbles in. Her blouse is torn, the side of her face scraped, and there's a boot print on her arm. David springs to his feet.

"Sophie!"

"Siddown!" Ariel barks. She cocks her pistol.

Ganymede staggers through the door behind Sophie. He's sloppy and inebriated, wagging a sawed-off shotgun. A look of astonishment passes over his face when he sees David in front of the open launch device. Ganymede shoves Sophie and she collapses into a chair. David rushes toward her.

"What has he done to you?"

"I'm okay, Davi—"

"Shut up!"

Ganymede smacks Sophie and she slumps forward. He points the shotgun at the back her head. David skids to a stop, his body trembling. He fantasizes about wrapping his fingers around Ganymede's veiny neck and wringing the life out of him.

"Ariel!" Ganymede rages. "What in hell's name is going on here?"

"I found Music Man here with the launch box open," she lies.

"That's right, freak," says David. "Huracan's wondrous plan is finished. The rocket's going to lift off, topple over and incinerate this quaint little Jonestown of yours. Guaranteed kill radius? A half mile. And that includes you and your bad fucking hair."

"Careful, you little pissant, "Ganymede replies. "The night is young. There's plenty of time to get what I need out of your little girlfriend. God, she is yummy."

He leans over and licks her face.

"You're disgusting," David seethes. "And she doesn't go for your type—a eunuch with makeup that looks like a pissed-on birthday cake."

"That's it, she's done."

Ganymede aims his sawed-off Browning at Sophie's stomach.

"Stop it!" Ariel shouts. "Now sit down, David."

But Wesson is on a roll. "I already switched the circuit out, loser. Party's over."

He holds up the golden SV-335 chip, which hasn't yet been installed. Ganymede seems to buy into his deception.

"Why you little scum. Is that right, Ariel?" He looks at her maniacally.

Now the moment of truth. Whose side will Ariel be on?

"Destroy it, David," Sophie shouts.

Ganymede slams her with the butt end of his gun. She clutches a hand to her ear to stave off a trickle of blood. David's anger has reached the breaking point, but Ariel brushes the Luger against the side of his head.

"Easy now, pretty boy," she coos in a sultry rasp, like a 1930s gangster moll: icy yet somehow strangely hot. "Time to switch that circuit back in."

David crosses his arms defiantly.

"I'm doin' nothin' ... until Roadrunner over there stands down."

A disbelieving smile creeps across Ganymede's face.

"Aww. So sweet," he says through pursed lips. "Big action hero wants to save 'the girl'.

Well, have it your way, but it would be far more merciful to put her out of her misery right here and now. Because when I'm done, you won't even recognize her." Ganymede giggles cruelly. "And then, it'll be your turn."

David looks at Ariel in disbelief.

"Really? And you call this nutcase 'brother'?"

"Just do it!" she shouts.

David begins to exchange the circuit, but suddenly becomes distracted by a powerful feeling. He glances across the room and sees Sophie's pale-green eyes blazing at him with inner confidence. *Be strong. The end is near,* they whisper.

Ganymede leans the shotgun against the wall. He walks to a communication console near the exit, picks up a hand-held mic and presses a button.

"Hey Arsehole. Audrius. Whatever your fuckin' name is. Report to Suite One immediately. Need escort. Do you read?"

A voice with a Russian accent crackles over the speaker.

"Roger that. But first, closing blast doors. Rocket is fueled."

"Just get over here, Com-rade," Ganymede replies in an exaggerated mock-Russian tone. "The guy's got the IQ of a plank."

He turns and faces David. "And how about you, hero boy? Almost finished? I'm really looking forward to slicing you up."

"It's done, goof. Here."

David tosses the exchanged computer circuit to Ganymede. It lands on the floor in front of the disciple.

"Mmm. So obedient. We could have had so much fun together."

"In your dreams!" Wesson replies, laughing aloud.

"I guess we won't be needing this anymore."

Ganymede stomps on the circuit board and it crunches into pieces. Ariel glances over at her 'brother' as she closes the launch case. David can sense that her anger has reached a rolling boil. He seems strangely confident, seeing that Ariel is unravelling.

"We need to get the launch case to Huracan on the yacht," Ariel says to her Greater God sibling. "On your feet, Wesson."

"Oh, you guys go on without me," Ganymede replies. He looks down at Sophie. "It's time to pluck some petals off this precious wildflower."

David grips the desk, ready to leap over it and take the mouthy bastard by the throat.

"It's time that Sophie and I went for our little walk on the pier." Ganymede pretends to tear up. "So sad. How the poor thing fell and snapped her neck on the rocks. Oh, boo hoo." He looks down at Sophie and licks his lips. "Now let's get a better look at you."

Ganymede tears the front of her blouse open. Three buttons pop off in succession, revealing the physique of a decathlete. Sophie's breasts heave up into her black sports bra, her sinewy thorax flexed. Sophie has a perfect body, though she'd be the first to refute that claim.

But Sophie doesn't flinch or cover up. After all, she's a warrior who's been training since the age of eight. This latest incident only serves to strengthen her resolve. Sophie Bisset has spent her entire life being underestimated by men. But she didn't become a captain, a top-of-class deepwater diver, an F-16 pilot, hand-to-hand combat and weapons expert by being a dainty pushover. Hell no. For Ganymede, it's just a matter of time. He's hoisting himself on his own petard just beautifully.

For David Wesson, though, it is time. Time to take Ganymede out. He flexes his leg muscles down to his toes and plots how he will jump over the desk, scramble across the floor and pull the feet out from under the crackpot– or meth head, or whatever the hell he is– then head-butt him to death. Trouble is, Ganymede is standing five feet away from the shotgun. But David's primal urge to protect Sophie is beyond all rational thought now.

"Easy, brother Ganymede," Ariel says. "We need to get these two on the yacht. *And we need to do it now!*" she screeches.

Oh, how siblings can fight! thinks David.

Ganymede inches toward Sophie.

"Your breasts are so lovely and firm. Let's have a looksee."

Suddenly, a crashing of elbows and the sound of knees hitting wood. Ganymede turns and sees David sprawled across the floor, wincing and gripping his elbow. The attack didn't go nearly as well as it had in his mind. Ganymede howls with laughter. The crazed minion feels so in charge that he doesn't even go for the shotgun. After all, Ariel has his back, right? He's free to have his way with Sophie whether David likes it or not. But as Ganymede reaches for her bra, a deafening shriek stops him cold.

"Ganymede! Stand. Down."

Ganymede faces Ariel, and finds himself staring down the barrel of her Luger. His mouth drops open. If it weren't for his garish makeup, one would see all color draining from his face.

"Sister?"

"Leave. Her. Alone," Ariel says, her voice as glacial as the bottle of rosé.

"Why you little skank!" Ganymede shouts.

Sophie takes advantage of his distraction. She somersaults out of her chair. David reaches for her, but she shoves him out of the way. She turns and faces Ganymede, who now looks like a mouse appetizer in front of two Komodo dragons.

"You stupid twat!" he says to Ariel. "You of all people won't mind if I have my way with this trashy tart. You've watched me a million times with other girls. You fuckin' *love it.*" He switches to a baby voice. "And what of the special times we had, sister?" He sticks his tongue out between makeup-smudged teeth and bats his eyes. Ariel responds by cocking the weapon and aiming it at his head, gripping the Luger with both hands in a stabilized position. Ganymede's grin dissolves into a shocked stare.

"First of all, you're not my real brother. In fact, none of this is real! This fake god, this fake religion, this fake everything! And another thing." Her voice drops to a deadly whisper: "Brothers don't treat sisters that way. That's not going to happen anymore, pig."

"You dirty whore. Gimme the gun."

He starts toward her, hand outstretched, but Ariel squeezes off a shot. It whizzes past Ganymede's head and blows a priceless Ming Dynasty vase into a million pieces. Ganymede ducks. He clenches his teeth and storms his cult-mate.

"Why you fucking cu—"

Suddenly, a sharp, pointed sound.

Pfeww. Followed by *splatt.* Ganymede looks down and sees blood oozing down his leg. He screams and grabs his crotch.

"You shot off my left nut, bitch!" he squeals.

Ariel stares at him with hellish ferocity.

"Oh yeah. That's right," she says. "You have ... two."

She targets the Luger a centimeter to the left and pulls the trigger. The bullet meets its mark, passing through hand and trouser, and blood and testicle matter splatter across the wall behind him. Ganymede crumples into a fetal position on the floor. Sophie walks up and stands over him as he grovels. The broken disciple looks at her, moaning and weeping.

"Aww. So sad. Now, what was it you said?" Sophie says with mock politeness.

"Ah yes. Oh... boo ... *HOO!*"

She kicks Ganymede full force in the face. His head buckles back, then recoils into the floor with equal fury. The disciple lies silent and limp as two pools of blood expand around him, one from his head and the other from his lower midsection.

David doesn't know quite how to react. He's lived through a number of anger episodes, mild by comparison with his ex-wife, but this truly confirms that hell hath no fury greater than *two* women scorned.

Chapter 38
Gravity

"That's correct, sir. We have full locks on Bird One and The Handler. Should be within a half-hour. Yes, I'm aware of that, General Passmore. No, we've not spoken with Ruthie directly. Hopefully there's some wiggle room if—" Ned McCarty holds the phone away from his ear then brings it back cautiously.

"I know you don't like the word 'hopefully', sir. Roger Wilco."

McCarty slams the phone down and picks up the ship's comm. "Collins. Tell Fisher to pull up anchor. Bring her in a half mile south of Breakwater. Quiet mode, no running lights."

"Roger that," Collins replies.

As Ariel marches Sophie and David toward the Breakwater Mansion's concrete pier, she clutches the control case in one hand and her Luger in the other. The disciple keeps her appearances up, for if she is discovered switching teams, this will surely be her last New Year. The morning sun is wide awake below the horizon and the wooded compound still alive with revelers in various stages of undress. Items of clothing are scattered through the trees and moans of pleasure echo through the forest.

"So why'd you flip sides?" David asks.

Ariel rolls her eyes. "You and your questions! If you must know, two reasons: immunity and, to be quite honest, money."

"Ah. So money talks and bullshit walks, eh?" Wesson replies as they approach Huracan's yacht.

"Plus, I've had enough weird sex here to last a lifetime. Make that two."

Sophie and David exchange a horrified glance.

"But now, it's time for you to pipe down, Wesson. I know that's not easy for you. I trust you have the tranq pistol?"

David frantically checks his pockets but comes up empty-handed.

"I have it, David," Sophie says.

Ariel can't resist another dig.

"Two words. Trai-ning."

Wesson is fed up with her hoity-toity attitude, but he suppresses a comeback. After all, she is holding a gun, and she did just blow another guy's balls off. At this juncture, every word, every micro-thought is critical. And David still doesn't know how they'll be getting out of here.

A hundred feet away, Audrius is standing beside the Lucky Tiger's roped-off gangway. He watches them with a dispassionate gaze, his ever-ready gun at his side.

"That's it. No sudden movements," Ariel advises as they approach the vessel.

"You know, your so-called brother is going to bleed out in that room," David says.

Ariel sighs.

"You are so not cut out for this business."

David glances back and raises an eyebrow.

"This business?"

Sophie's elbow jams into the soft tissue below his rib cage.

"Smarten up, David!"

"Hallelujah to that," Ariel says.

Wesson instantly cools his jets. After witnessing the brutal emasculation of Ganymede, he realizes there's never been a better time to just shut up and obey these alpha women.

When they reach the Lucky Tiger, Ariel passes the launch case to Audrius.

"Where Brutus?" the gunman asks in his thick Russian accent.

"Brutus is drunk," Ariel replies. "Got into the vodka."

She glances over her shoulder.

"There he is."

Fifty feet behind them, Audrius's hench-mate is wobbling like a wino under the effect of the tranquilizer drug. He smells like a distillery and looks like he's pissed his pants. Back at Huracan's suite, after shooting Brutus with the dart gun then locking the bleeding Ganymede in the hidden room, Ariel doused the security goon with vodka as he drifted back into consciousness. She then handed him the half-empty bottle, which he now clutches at his side. His shirt and jacket are drenched, a sloppy grin plastered across his bobbing red face. After every few paces he stops and takes a swig, and if anyone comes close, he salutes them, then bows and shakes their hand.

"Durak!" Audrius curses in Russian. "Brutus very bad drunk. Plus, stupid cretin, he drink Polish vodka."

Audrius spits on the ground, disgusted that his cohort is consuming non-Russian vodka. "Slaboumnyy!" he shouts.

Brutus looks over, places his hands under his armpits and flaps his elbows like a chicken.

Audrius shoves Sophie and David across the footbridge onto the yacht.

Crime does pay, David thinks, shocked by the ship's elegance and size.

"Stop," Audrius commands. He enters a code on a keypad and a glass door slides open. "Now go."

Sophie and David enter a lavish stateroom, where they find Huracan seated atop his throne. The leader shoos out a group of disciples who are gathered before him. Audrius approaches Huracan and places the launch case on a small side table as the disciples bow and hurry out the door.

"So. You two are alive. How delightful," Huracan says through a forced smile.

He claps his hands feebly, then turns toward Ariel.

"Where is Ganymede? I need my medication."

"He's off in the forest with some young thing," Ariel replies.

"Why must he always disappoint me so?" Huracan glances at a set of I Ching coins then looks up vacantly.

"The oracle has foretold me of your vile intentions, David. But sadly, you have failed. And now, you must die. But you both shall serve me well in the afterlife, for eternity and beyond. Audrius, take the girl outside and await my execution order."

Audrius pulls a bowie knife from an ankle sheath and moves toward Sophie, but David steps in front of her and blocks his way.

"Leave her, Huracan. Take my life, not hers."

The gunman is mystified by David's selfless bravery. He turns toward Huracan as a smile stretches across the Reverend's taut lips.

"Oh, David. Imagine that. So impressive! And here I thought you were just another *stupid musician.*" His thin nose wrinkles as he says it.

"You don't have to do this, *Nathaniel,*" Sophie says.

Huracan winces. The mention of his real name seems to cause him physical pain. He raises a shaky hand to his forehead.

"That name is not permitted here," he grumbles.

"What happened to that caring young man I once knew? The shy altar boy who always wore a smile. Nathaniel Klement. Yes. That's your name."

Huracan covers his ears. His pronounced cheekbones look as if they're going to tear through the skin. "That name died a long time ago, foolish child. When I became a God."

"You're sick, Nathaniel. You need help. I know your father was cruel to you."

"You know?!" Huracan springs to his feet. "You *know* my father was cruel? No, you don't know, you spoiled daddy's girl. How I was whipped like a dog after I found my Asian mother face down in a swamp. How I lived under the floorboards and was forced to kill at age nine for his perverse pleasure. You know nothing!"

Huracan opens the briefcase.

"Uh, careful with that," David advises.

"Where is that fool Ganymede? Why must he abandon me? I need."

"See? It's the drugs, Nathaniel," Sophie says. "They've messed up your mind."

Huracan inserts a key into the right side of the control surface.

"You don't have to do this, Huracan," David says, but Audrius elbows him out of the way and puts Sophie in a chokehold.

"Why can no one understand?" Huracan cries, tears welling in his eyes. "Nathaniel

Klement died ten thousand millennia ago. Can't you see? The great Huracan is *saving* humanity. Rebirth must always begin with death. And you two could have joined me, become gods like me."

His expression ices.

"But you, David Wesson, you dare to stop me? Sacrifice your insignificant life to save humanity and this foolish girl? Pathetic!"

He stares at David with hollow, unfeeling eyes.

"There is no reason to fear death. You are already dead. I am the only one truly alive in this kingdom. My kingdom! Death is merely an amusement."

Huracan turns to his henchman.

"Audrius. Take the girl outside and kill her."

The gunman forces Captain Bisset toward the door while Ariel keeps her pistol trained on David, who now knows that the only way to save Sophie will be to sacrifice his own life.

"No, Huracan!" David shouts. "Sophie, don't even think about going out that door."

"Ariel. Give me your key," Huracan commands.

Ariel looks drained of every elegant molecule, concerned only about what's best for her. She seems terrified and unsure of how to proceed— until a voice echoes out of a doorway beyond Huracan.

"Give it to him, Ariel."

The blunt end of a pistol sneaks out of the darkened entranceway, followed by a short mustachioed man wearing rose-colored glasses, sequined pants and a porkpie hat. The Reverend settles back in his chair and begins arming the launch device.

"So, you are more than just a terrible singer, Reggie," David says, wishing for a moment that he could take back the word 'terrible'. "Or should I call you Ennio?"

Reggie wags his gun at Ariel. "Give the reverend your key, 'sister'. And drop your weapon." Ariel swallows drily. She opens her mouth to speak. "Don't. Even. Bother," Reggie growls.

Ariel is without words. She places the Luger at her feet, then removes the key from a lanyard around her neck. Huracan snatches it greedily and inserts it into the second slot. He begins typing a code on the briefcase's numeric keypad.

Ariel, her face ashen and lower lip quivering, raises her hands over her head. Reggie turns to Audrius and, in a flawless Muscovite dialect, orders him to take the girl outside.

"Voz'mi devushku na ulitsu," he says.

Audrius pushes Sophie out the door and slams it behind them.

"Huracan! Stop this madness!" David turns toward the exit but freezes when he hears the sound of Reggie's pistol being racked.

"I'm a good shot, David Wesson. Just like you," the rogue agent warns. "One more step and I'll cut you in half. Nothing would give me greater pleasure than to watch you die. Continue the sequence, Reverend."

Huracan twists the keys clockwise. A string of lights begins to pulsate. Huracan flips up a safety latch that reveals a large red button. David hears the sounds of a skirmish outside: Sophie yelling, Audrius grunting, bodies hitting the door. David is trapped, unable to move.

"Don't do it, Huracan!" he shouts.

But the Reverend is a man possessed now, seemingly devoid of all human emotion. He raises a trembling finger over the launch button.

"Ten minutes. Right, Ennio?" he says without looking up.

"Correct. We'll be safely to sea by then."

Keeping his gun aimed at David, Reggie peels off his fake moustache and tosses it to the floor. He removes his porkpie cap and replaces it with a sea captain's hat. David prepares to rush him, knowing full well it will be the last thing he does on this earth. Huracan looks up callously.

"You must be careful what you die for, David."

"No, Huracan!"

The outside door swishes open. A volley of gunfire explodes past Huracan's head, narrowly missing Reggie, who turns and vanishes into the shadows.

"Not so fast, FREAK!" Sophie shouts.

Crouched and battle-ready by the exit door, drenched in sweat in her camo tights and athletic bra, her teeth bared like a wild panther, Sophie aims a TEC-9 automatic at Huracan's head. At her feet, Audrius crawls by, a look of confusion on his face. The muscle-bound Russian pulls a tranquilizer dart out of his shoulder, then his eyes cross as he loses muscle control and collapses to the floor. Huracan glares at Captain Bisset as his finger caresses the launch button, which is now flashing. A cruel smile widens across the Reverend's face. He forces the button down.

"No!" David howls.

A concussion shakes the room as a cloud of acrid smoke spews out of ceiling vents. Simultaneously, a trap door opens beneath Huracan. His throne collapses and gravity pulls him through a hole in the floor. The throne springs back to its original shape and the door snaps shut beneath it, leaving no hint that the Reverend was even there. Alarms start blaring and a large wall-mounted LED flashes to life, with numbers that make an ominous beep as every second slips away.

10:00, 09:59, 09:58 ...

Chapter 39
Not A Drill

"Proceed to north end of the compound. This is not a drill. Do not panic. Proceed to north end of the ..."

The message repeats ad nauseam, its Orwellian voice barely audible over screams and the whooping of alarms. Confused stragglers join a stream of cult members migrating north. Onboard the Lucky Tiger, Sophie and David are stunned by Huracan's ingenious escape. David cups his hand to his mouth and shouts at the floor where the Reverend sat a minute ago.

"Full marks for that one, Huracan! Sophie, let's get the hell out of— Whoa."

Outside, the chatter of machine-gun fire, dangerously close by.

"Here. The tranq pistol!" Captain Bisset shouts.

She tosses the CO2 gun to David, who takes a look at the meagre armament and turns to Ariel.

"Mind if I borrow your Luger?"

"As if!" the frazzled diva replies. "Gotta look out for number one, baby." Ariel races out the door, her long ponytail in tow.

Sophie creeps toward the exit with Audrius' gun in front of her as the Lucky Tiger's engines thunder to life. Outside, a stone-on-stone rumbling noise sounds like an earthquake. Automatic gunfire is yards away now. Sophie targets the stateroom's opening and David crouches behind her, his pistol ready. After another volley of shots from outside, a gun-toting male bursts through the doorway.

"Don't shoot!"

"Drago!" David shouts.

Sophie almost collapses as she disengages.

"X! You're still alive! Oh, thank God. Sophie? Nice to see you too."

"Drago, you lanky lout. I love you!" David exclaims.

"What's that rumbling sound, Drago?" Sophie says. "And where's the small-arms fire coming from?"

"Sorry, Captain Bisset, the gunfire was me. The other thing? You better come see. We have to leave. Now!"

Drago bolts out the door. He blasts an arc of bullets into the sky, causing more screams to ring out across the compound. Terrified stevedores cast off the launch's mooring ropes and run for their lives. As David crosses the ship's gangway, he sees a twenty-foot-wide chunk of concrete sliding open on the dock in front of him. Drago is yards away from the widening crevice as he helps Sophie.

"Don't stop, X!"

The yacht suddenly lurches forward, engines raging. Sophie grabs David's arm and pulls him ashore as the footbridge tears away. He narrowly avoids getting his leg shorn off by twisting metal. David stares into the rocket silo and the devil incarnate seems to gleam back at him. Drago, already at the far side of the dock, waves furiously at David.

"Hurry!" he shouts.

Just then, a roar assaults their eardrums from just above the treetops.

"F-18s!" Sophie yells.

David knows that if the sound were from an F-18, they'd already be dead. He recognizes the unmistakable whine of an A-10 Thunderbolt, a close-support aircraft. It must be making a warning pass. David considers himself lucky: a warning from an A-10 is rare. He realizes that the Breakwater Estate is seconds away from an airstrike. David follows Sophie across the shuddering concrete, where Drago helps them half slide, half fall down the six-foot drop on the other side. Sophie checks her compass, then motions for the men to follow her. She sets off through the tangled mangrove roots.

"Go, X!" Drago shouts.

Drago follows them and watches David's back as they storm through the brush. They arrive at an ocean inlet, where a giant of a man dressed in camo and a balaclava awaits. Despite their checkered history, David is overjoyed to see Mr. Pong. The big Samoan grabs Sophie and tosses her into a rigid-inflatable that looks to be twenty-five feet long. The boat is powered by a pair of jet-black outboard engines.

Captain Bisset scurries to the bow and lies down, her gun pointed forward. David feels a hand on his belt, and in an instant, he too is flying headfirst into the boat. He bounces and scrapes across the carbon-fiber floor. Pong scrambles into the driver's seat, where he fires the engines up as Drago wades into the shallows. Drago pushes the boat to deeper water, then rolls in and faces backwards, providing aft cover. Pong guns the throttle and the boat accelerates as if powered by rockets. The inflatable screams out of the inlet into an open bay.

For a fleeting moment, David manages to compartmentalize his fear. He's dreamt of riding on one these go-fasts since he first saw one at age thirteen, when his father was stationed with the Pacific Fleet at Coronado. To think that he is part of this elite squadron is an adrenalin rush like no other. Now, if it was only just a game. Or *is war the deadliest of all games?* he wonders.

The strong but silent giant handles the inflatable vessel as if it were an extension of his own body. He constantly adjusts the tilt of the engines to keep the props under the surface at precisely the right angle for maximum speed and control. David pops his head up, and sees a large motor launch hurtling toward them. Alarmed, he glances back at Mr. Pong, but the Samoan's eyes stay riveted. The launch pulls out in front of them, thankfully going in the same direction, but much slower than they are.

"Hang tight!" Sophie shouts.

David bounces into the air as the Zodiac hurtles over the ship's wake. Pong dials the twin 250s back, narrowly avoiding a collision with the larger vessel. David looks up and sees Lady Argon written in cursive lettering on the boat's transom. The Lady's rear door folds down and Crewman Fisher helps Sophie aboard.

"Go. Go. Go!" Drago yells at David.

David scrambles in a four-limbed drive to the Zodiac's bow, slowing only to pick up the tranquilizer pistol that has fallen from his pocket. "Leave it," Drago shouts, but David grabs the CO_2 gun and shoves its barrel loosely into his pocket as Fisher pulls him aboard.

Drago follows them onboard, then pushes on the bow of the Zodiac, which sends it veering off. David turns to watch and is met by a propeller wash that blasts his face like a firehose on steroids. He wipes his eyes and looks out at Pong, whose balaclava is pulled up on his forehead. Pong feigns an innocent shrug, then he makes a grimacing warrior face. He points at David, forms a fist and pounds his chest with it. Wesson allows himself a proud grin as Mr. Pong slams the throttle down and the craft vanishes in a wash of rooster-tail spray.

"Hang tight!" Fisher bellows.

The Lady Argon bears down as it hurtles toward the open sea.

The A-10 fighter roars past, a hundred feet off the bow, its twin turbofan engines bombarding the team's ears. The aircraft's wings twitch and it angles away dropping flares. David and Sophie cling to the gunnels and make their way amidships, where they find Ned seated on a swiveling chair with the missile's control surface on his lap.

"For Christ's sake! We're the good guys," Ned screams into a handheld mic. "Tell that A-10 of yours to back off! You tell General Passmore that he's threatening the entire mission with this airstrike foolishness. We have full control locks on Bird One, goddamn it!"

Ned concludes his tirade by throwing the microphone with a whipping motion. It stretches out on its curly cord then recoils with equal fury, nearly bonking him between the eyes. Ned turns and sees Sophie and David standing behind him.

"Sorry about that, guys. Goddamned bureaucrats!" He shakes his fist at the horizon. Ned reaches down and retrieves the mic. "Collins, full stop. Engines on idle. Bow point northeast. No anchor."

"Roger, Commander," Collins's voice crackles.

"What happens now, Commander McCarty?" Sophie asks.

"Thanks to my brilliant design, it's quite simple," he announces. Sophie can barely suppress gagging at his superior attitude. "We're now locked into the missile's guidance control, thanks to you two. Now, using these three toggles" —Ned tips the control surface so David can see— "I'm going to fly the missile ten miles offshore and destroy it there."

"You're going to detonate a nuclear warhead?!"

"No David. The warhead will self-arm when it reaches twenty thousand feet. There's zero risk of an atomic blast according to my calculations, unless it carries on through twenty thousand."

"And if that happens?" David asks.

"It won't," Ned replies smartly. "I'm going to detonate her west of here at nineteen thousand by pushing the red button at the bottom right." McCarty points at a numbered readout that indicates 0:0:0:0. "This is the altimeter, now at zero since the rocket is at sea level." He motions toward the upper center of the rectangular control panel. "The solid-green light indicates that we are locked into the missile's guidance control. If it starts flashing or turns red, we've lost sync."

"What then?" David asks, leaning in for a closer look.

"Part of the circuit you installed is a fail-safe, which means that without our input, the missile will self-destruct at twenty three thousand. But that could place it right above us, where the explosive concussion and debris would be substantial. Plus, there could be"—McCarty clears his throat nervously— "radioactive fallout," he says, his voice suddenly dry and hoarse. The Coast Guard has secured a two-hundred-square-mile safe zone east of here, and that's where I'm going to blow it up, or crash it into the sea. So, in answer to your question, David, pray that there isn't a 'what then'."

David knows that Ned is a genius, but it seems too great a possibility that something will go wrong.

"Hur-a-kane must have got away on his mini-sub," Drago interjects.

"Mini-sub? I doubt it," Ned replies. "But if he did, the submersible and Lucky Tiger will likely rendezvous with that Russian sub northeast of here. Not our problem."

"So the Russians are behind all this?" David says.

Ned cocks his head and gives David a 'don't ask' look.

"How long before liftoff?" Sophie asks.

Just then, a low tone squawks out of the control box and a row of green and red lights starts blinking.

"Okay, gang. I need quiet now."

McCarty flips an array of switches and settles back into his chair. He looks up over his shoulder as a six-foot-diameter radar dish atop the flying bridge spins and locks onto the launch site.

Sophie, bruised and bloodied, reaches for David. She slips her trembling hand into his. David has never seen her so frail. She gazes up at him, her soft green eyes damp with emotion. Strong and brave Captain Bisset looks like a frightened little girl.

"Hey," David says, "don't forget. Popcorn. My place, right?"

He pulls her in close, then looks off to sea, suddenly fighting his own emotions. Ned takes a deep breath.

"All right, kids. Showtime."

Chapter 40
Apocalyptic Fury

An apocalyptic fury of red-orange smoke billows out of Huracan's underground silo. From the team's offshore vantage point, it's like watching an erupting volcano. David is dumbstruck. He'd been hoping, praying, that the missile would fail to launch, but that option has expired. Ned clutches two of the three control device toggles, his eyes locked on the expanding plume. He motions urgently at David.

"Left stick controls engine thrust," McCarty says, speaking uncharacteristically quickly. "Right adjusts the direction vanes. The all-important middle toggle determines the—"

Ned is silenced by a concussion of engine noise as it tears across the ship's deck. The blast is deafening, even after travelling two miles over open sea at the speed of sound. David is so focused on Ned's briefing, that every muscle tenses when the shock wave hits. His foot catches an errant coil of line on the deck and he stumbles.

"No, X!" Drago shouts from behind him. "Watch out for the—"

David feels the tranquilizer pistol squeezing out of his pocket. He reaches down to shove it back in, but his hand catches the gun's handgrip and sends it spinning end over end toward the deck. A thought terrorizes David: *Did I put the safety on?* His question is soon answered as the pistol smacks into the wooden floorboard and discharges with a *pop* sound. Simultaneously, Ned slaps his neck as if he's been bitten by a horsefly. The missile lifts out of its underground housing and a blinding orange rocket engine flame appears as it clears the dock. McCarty plucks a tiny tranquilizer dart out of his neck and a puzzled look creeps across his face.

He slumps into his seat, unconscious.

"Holy shit!" David shouts.

"Ned!"

Sophie rushes over and shakes Ned, but he just moans and smiles stupidly.

"X! Look!" Drago shouts.

The missile, now fully airborne, is accelerating skyward, although it looks to be struggling to gain altitude.

"It's running heavy," Sophie shouts. She pulls Ned out of his chair.

"Right on, man," he babbles.

David rushes to the control device and looks down at its array of blinking lights and switches.

"My kid's got a toy truck with a controller something like this."

"Good god," Drago moans, his face pale. He reaches into his pocket and pulls out his rosary.

David nudges the left toggle up. The missile reacts by picking up speed and blasting toward a thin layer of clouds.

"Not that one!" Drago shouts. "Ned! Wake up."

David eases the lever back and the engine flame shortens. The missile slows to a hover, then begins slipping earthward toward Huracan's estate.

"Damn!" David exclaims. "Is Ned awake or what?"

Sophie shakes Ned by the shoulders. She slaps him across the face.

"Par-ty," he mumbles through a sloppy grin.

David throttles the engine up again. The rocket slows before it reaches the pier, but its nose suddenly topples toward them. David pushes on the right-side control, but the missile starts drifting in their direction, two hundred feet above the water, riding a blast furnace of flame. David forces the lever up, but that causes the off-kilter rocket to pick up speed toward them,

"X! Try the middle controller!" Drago shouts.

"What does it do?" David shouts back.

"I don't know!"

The roar of the engine crescendos as the missile hurtles toward them.

"Roll it!" Sophie shouts.

"What?" David replies.

"The middle stick rolls the missile. Do it now!"

David flips the middle lever to the left. Nothing. Drago starts reciting scripture. David grinds his teeth, presses the middle lever up as high as it will go and adds some thrust. The rocket arcs upward and passes over them, so close that the team can feel its blistering heat.

"I didn't need those eyebrows anyway," David says as the fuel-laden beast roars off in a northerly direction.

"Don't hit our billion-dollar submarine out there," Ned slurs. "General Passmore's not going to be hap-py."

Ned giggles. He points a wobbly hand to sea and raises his middle finger.

A distorted voice howls over the ship's public address system: *"McCarty! What the hell are you doing? There's a goddamn Ohio-class sub out here!"*

David starts flicking randomly at the control levers, but the missile stays on a northward trajectory toward the ocean research school at Fonfar Station. Crewman Fisher spots something at sea.

"Ship ahoy!" he shouts.

David squints and sees a motor launch speeding away, three miles north of them. The missile is losing altitude, headed straight for it.

"It's Hur-a-kane's boat!" Drago yells. "I wouldn't want to be on that right now."

Wesson toys with the levers and the rocket's flame rakes across the Lucky Tiger, incinerating the thirty-million-dollar ship's front end.

"I think I'm getting the hang of this," David says,

Drago begins to recite a Hail Mary.

"That's not helping!" David snipes.

The Slovenian ceases his invocation mid-sentence.

"Fly it east and drop it in the ocean. Over there," says Sophie, pointing eastward as she steadies Ned.

"Woo-hoo!" McCarty shouts.

"If only it were that easy," David complains.

Just then, the ship's speaker comes alive with the sound of an emotive Russian voice.

"Eto akt voyny! If missile comes closer, we will initiate counter-strike."

"Counter-strike this!" Ned yells, grabbing his crotch. "Goddamned Russkies. Shouldn't be out there anyway!"

David exchanges a bewildered glance with Sophie. This loud-mouthed tough-guy routine is completely out of character for the usually reserved and in-control Ned.

"You can do it, David!" Sophie shouts.

David invokes a prayer as he finesses the controls, trying to tap into any higher power that might be listening. The rocket seems to respond to his salutation and begins to gain altitude. He's finally able to nudge it toward the safety zone.

"Where's the self-destruct button?"

"Ned said it's on the lower right, right?" Sophie replies, her answer more of a question.

"That'd be it," Ned adds, slurring, "but you might be needing this." McCarty grins as he swings a key back and forth on a cord.

"Jeezuz, Ned! Stop fu—" David stops himself from completing the sentence. "Sophie! Get the key. It must go above the kill switch."

She retrieves it and rushes to David, who is struggling to stay in control of both the missile and himself. She inserts the key in the slot.

"Do I turn it to the right, Ned?"

"That's what *I'd* do," he replies in a smarty-pants kind of way.

"Go ahead, Soph. I got this," David says. "Just a bit more thrust."

As Sophie twists the key, the green light at top center suddenly turns red. A buzzing sound begins squawking out of the control box.

"We've lost sync!" Sophie shouts.

The rocket trips into a violent spiral, its nose pointed forward and its tail circling itself, creating a Spirographic smoke effect. David toys with the controls, but nothing. The antenna dish is stuck, pointing the wrong way. He shouts up to the flying bridge.

"Collins! Bring the bow thirty degrees south."

"Yes, sir!"

Collins swings the Lady Argon around. The team are nearly thrown off their feet. Ned thinks it's the funniest thing ever. The radar dish begins to track again as an angry voice bellows through the loudspeaker.

"Jesus H. Christ, McCarty! What the hell are you doing? End this now! Do you read? If this goes bad ... you're finished! We're all goddamned finished."

McCarty looks out to sea, puts his thumbs in his ears and makes a loud farting sound with his lips. The rocket roars eastward, stuck in its spiral. Sophie eyes the controls while David focuses on the out-of-control missile.

"We have lock!" she shouts. "I repeat. We have lock."

"Let's finish this!" David says, sweat dripping into his eyes. "Will you do the honors, m'lady?"

"Hellya!"

Sophie punches the red button. It begins to pulse and the control box starts emitting a loud beeping sound. Everyone stares at rocket, but nothing.

"Ned? This thing's not going to go nuclear, right?"

McCarty flips David off.

"Nah," he says, then, *"Five, four ..."*

Everyone joins in. *"Three, two ..."*

The missile starts falling. Pieces begin breaking off. The fuselage starts folding into itself.

"One!"

A fireball blows out to a mile in diameter, perfectly placed in the safe zone. Trails of debris rain down in every direction as molten chunks plummet into the ocean. The team also explodes, with shouts, hugs and a few tears. General Passmore's voice erupts over the ship's speaker.

"McCarty, you're a goddamn genius! I don't know how you pulled this off, but I'm going to pin a medal on you myself! And Ruthie, the rest of the VFS team? We couldn't have done it without you. God and the free world thank you. Passmore out."

David lays the control box on Ned's chair. He turns and lifts Sophie off her feet. Both are fighting tears of joy. After a long embrace, David lets her slip back to the deck. She pulls him in close. That's when David spots Mr. Pong standing amidships. And he has a guest with him— a desperately thin older man, dressed in a tweed suit, with a Windsor-cut collar and gray tie.

"Dad!" Sophie shouts.

"Gilbert's your... dad?"

Sophie rushes over to him. Gilbert is overcome with emotion. He holds her tightly.

"Oh, my little girl. I never should have got you into this business. But you loved it so much, there was nothing I could do to stop you!"

Sophie turns and motions at David.

"I know you've met," she says, "but— Dad, David. David, Dad."

Gilbert reaches out and gives David a firm handshake. "Thank you, son. And thanks to all of you for taking care of my precious Sophie."

David is speechless at the revelation that Gilbert is Sophie Bisset's father. But in retrospect, it makes sense. How Gilbert asked David to take care of "my precious Sophie." How she talked about her father being a "legendary agent." How they grew up on the island, the family tragedy, the helicopter pilotry and all the Ruthie vehicles.

Crewman Fisher walks up to David. "Beer?"

"Oh yes."

Fisher hands him a frosty Kalik.

David, about to guzzle it back, notices that things seem to be strangely quiet. He turns and sees the team standing in a half-circle. Everyone is staring at him. Everyone, that is, except Ned, who is curled up on the deck, snoring.

"I'd like to make a toast... *to David Wesson,*" Sophie shouts. Nice job, David. It's been a pleasure working with you."

The team join in with their own praises, but David feels awkward being the center of attention.

"Well," he says, "not bad for my first day on the job, I suppose."

"To David Wesson first day on job." Drago says.

"Hear! Hear!" the legendary agent shouts.

Sophie approaches David. They tap their bottles together and take a long, cool swig. She snuggles in close.

"Hey! Easy, girl. Your dad's right there."

"Something tells me he approves of you."

"Really? His daughter ... *with a musician?*"

Sophie punches him lovingly and they walks to the far side of the ship, where a navy frigate and a coast guard cutter are arriving. To the north, a giant submarine is steaming toward the crash site. Sophie and David look out over the debris, some of it still trickling from the sky and splashing into the sea. Somehow, it's all strangely romantic. David looks into her misty eyes.

"You know, I think I've fallen in—"

Sophie places her finger over his lips. She pulls him in tightly. As they kiss, their bodies seem to melt into each other.

Collins lets off a horn blast from the Lady Argon. The frigate responds with a whoop of its siren, and the A-10 screams past wagging its wings. But Sophie and David, lost in their own private universe, no longer hear a thing except their own hearts beating. They surpassed the odds and made it out alive. And so alive.

Chapter 41
Dawn Of A New Day

David reclines near the bow of a Zodiac dinghy piloted by Captain Sophie. A half mile behind them, Ned's launch is steaming toward the debris field. A smoky cloud is still dissipating, and all manner and size of vessels are off their port bow.

"You'd think that Pong would let us use his real boat."

Sophie slows the engine.

"Huh?"

"He could have at least tidied up. Look at all this crud."

David points to a scattering of tackle and a stringer of fish. He picks up a loaded spearfishing gun.

"Whoa!" Sophie ducks. "I trust the safety's on."

"Yeah, yeah. Rub it in." David double-checks the trigger mechanism. He lays the gun down. "I hope Ned's okay."

"Oh I don't think Ned's feeling any pain," Sophie replies.

They share a laugh at Ned's expense, reminiscing about his bizarre antics and incorrigible, drug-fueled disdain for authority.

"No kidding! Quite the rebel under that Mr. Rogers exterior."

"He'd make a terrible druggie," Sophie adds.

David watches as a massive Sea Stallion helicopter arrives over the crash site. Divers start jumping out of it.

"Just like the movies. The cavalry shows up after we do the dirty work."

Sophie nods her head.

"Trust me. It's always like that."

It's surprisingly warm for a January morning. Fluffy clouds drift over the turquoise sea toward the gleaming sands of Marlin Cay, where David was learning scuba only yesterday.

"I can't believe I've only known you for two days," he says.

"It's been a blur."

"I hated saying goodbye to everybody. Especially Drago. He was all choked-up. I felt like Dorothy saying goodbye to the Tin Man."

Sophie laughs.

"For a mercenary, he's a surprisingly sensitive character. I've been on missions with him before. He's a good man to have watching your six."

"I'll say. And Gilbert being your dad? Unreal."

Sophie kills the engine and lets the boat drift. She tilts her head back to catch some sun and listen to the sound of lapping waves. David finds himself staring at her as the ocean breeze rustles her soft blond hair. He's so turned on by her confidence and strength, yet at the same time she has a fun-loving, little-girl quality. He prays he'll get a chance to know Sophie better, because something about her feels so right. David wants to believe the feelings are mutual, but he's been stung before.

"By the way," he says. "I have to ask: Who was that tall dude with the sunken cheeks at the bus stop?"

"What?"

"The guy who stole your computer case – or should I say – the guy you switched computer cases with? I followed him to the church."

"That's a little above your pay grade, David, but seeing as you just saved the world. And you do have a level three security clearance…"

David points a finger at Sophie. "There is that."

"He was a new recruit. Not my choice, by the way. Only he screwed up his first mission. If he got on the bus like he was supposed to, he'd still be alive."

A graveyard chill falls over David as he digests what Sophie is saying.

"You don't think it's because I followed him that he ended up—"

"You can't blame yourself, David."

"I guess that answers that question."

"These things happen."

David is horrified that he may have contributed to Aaden's death. At the same time, seeing and hearing Sophie's stark reaction is a reminder of what different worlds they come from.

"Anyway, the tide is low. I'll take us around the far side of the island. Skeleton Bay is over there." She points and David looks west, where the resort's long wooden dock beckons. He notices a boat approaching them.

"Someone you know?"

"Probably Tony."

"Looks familiar. Does Tony have a wooden boat?"

Sophie looks out at the vessel. "No. That's not his. Anyway, we better get going."

She fires up the Zodiac's twenty-five-horsepower engine and shifts it into gear. David looks back and sees a series of three quick flashes from the vessel's spotlight. The bow of the boat lifts up then lowers. Then the sound of two toots from the boat's horn.

"I think it is Tony," David says. "We'd better see what he wants."

Sophie holds their engine at a trolling speed. She looks over her shoulder. As the boat gets closer, it begins to look familiar.

"Wait a sec. That's—"

A series of tiny flashes from the approaching boat are followed almost instantaneously by metallic ricocheting and the sound of air hissing from the Zodiac's inflatable hull.

"Huracan's boat!" David exclaims.

Sophie twists the throttle, but the engine coughs. A multicolored pool of oil is oozing out of its lower unit. Huracan's yacht-tender throttles up and bears down on them. Another burst of gunfire snaps by.

Sophie looks down and sees fuel dripping from a hole in the gas line. She covers it with her thumb and starts pumping on the priming bulb, but the engine sputters and dies. Huracan's boat is hurtling toward them at full speed now. Sophie pulls repeatedly on the starter cord and the engine coughs to life. She twists the throttle and the Zodiac jerks forward, narrowly avoiding being cut in half by the launch as it roars past them at thirty miles an hour without changing direction. Its wake slams into Sophie and David's boat, nearly tossing them into the sea.

"What the hell!" David watches as the vessel speeds off, spewing smoke out of its twin exhaust pipes.

"Our engine and fuel line have been hit," Sophie shouts. "We've got to get to Marlin Cay."

The engine knocks and shudders, but Sophie keeps it going.

"Damn!" David shouts. "It's coming around again."

The launch starts a wide, sweeping turn, then arcs to the right and zeroes in on them.

Another scattering of gunfire whistles past. Sophie twists the throttle, but even if the Zodiac's engine were running at full capacity, it would still be disadvantaged against the approaching behemoth. Sophie coaxes the inflatable back up to speed and starts pushing and pulling on the engine tiller in a zigzagging maneuver.

"Hold on! We'll be harder to hit this way. Who the hell is it?"

David looks back at the launch, which is two hundred feet away and closing. A solitary figure stands up behind the steering wheel.

"Huracan!"

Sophie veers right, but she can't shake him. Soon, the Baby Tiger is almost on top of them.

"Hang on!" Sophie shouts.

David grips a handhold and the bottom of his seat at the same time. Sophie cranks the motor left. Huracan roars past them, but the wide-beamed vessel brushes the side of their inflatable. David is flung into the sea. Mid-air, he locks a stare on the diabolical cult leader. Huracan grins psychotically, his bleached white teeth glinting in the sunlight. The sound of high-pitched laughter sweeps past as David plunges into the ocean.

When he surfaces, he sees that Huracan's boat is coming around for another pass. He feels a nudge on the back of his shoulder— the bow of the inflatable.

"Get in! Sophie shouts. "Grab two handholds at the same time."

It takes every scrap of strength, but David pulls himself up and sloshes onto the gasoline-soaked floor. Sophie guns the stammering engine as Huracan lines up behind them again. It's like a World War I dogfight, except Sophie and David are in a lumbering civilian craft and Huracan is Baron von Richthofen in a venomous Fokker.

"I'm going to take us into the shallows," Sophie shouts. "The coral is sharp like glass in there. Do not fall out."

She aims the bow toward the south side of Marlin Cay. Soon, coral heads are whizzing past under the surface. David glances down and sees the speargun. He reaches for it as Sophie resumes her zigzagging pattern, but the engine starts coughing again. David slides onto the floor and the gun almost washes past him, but he's finally able to wrap his fingers around its long shaft. He props himself into a reverse seated position up front and flips the safety off.

"On my command, stop zigzagging and drive toward Marlin Cay," David shouts.

"What?"

"*When I say so,*" he yells, even louder to be heard above the engine noise, "*drive in a straight line. Then prepare to make a sharp left. Okay?*

"*Got it!*" Sophie shouts.

David braces himself on the Zodiac's bow as Huracan's craft looms behind them. David raises the speargun into position, but as he fine-tunes his aim, bullets spray up the port side. A jolt of red-hot pain explodes into his left shoulder.

"Aaaah! The bastard got me! Oh that hurts."

David looks up and sees Huracan laughing. The Reverend even slows his launch, as if planning to toy with his injured prey before delivering the inevitable coup de grâce. But after a few meagre seconds, the cult leader throttles up and the bow of the Baby Tiger slams down at full speed.

"Hang on, David! Focus! You're going to be okay."

Knives of pain stab the length of David's arm as he struggles to raise the spear-gun into position. He tilts it up like a longbow, grimacing as blood seeps from his shoulder.

"Now!" David yells.

Sophie stops zig-zagging and aims their boat toward the island. David makes a series of calculations and tries to tap into his youthful distance-shooting crown of old. There will be only one chance. David squeezes the trigger and the three-foot-long spear takes flight on an upward trajectory. But will it be too high and overshoot? Or will it be too low and bounce harmlessly off the windshield? Even if it's an inch wide of its target, all will be lost.

Huracan fails to catch sight of the projectile until he spots its glint over the gunwales. He twists his body, but it's too late. The barbed metal skewer plunges into his throat.

"Hard left!" David shouts.

Sophie yanks the tiller and the Zodiac hairpins out of Huracan's way. He roars past them, gagging, clutching his pierced neck as the launch hurtles toward the shoals. Struggling to dislodge the spear from his windpipe, the Reverend loses his grip on the steering wheel. His boat careens at full speed toward a two-foot-high rock abutment.

Sophie kills the engine and rushes forward to stop the flow of blood from David's shoulder.

"You got him, David! You got him! Stay with me."

David's eyes look like giant saucers. His head is swaying, his skin clammy and pale. He gasps as Sophie puts pressure on his wound. She knows she's hurting him by compressing the injury, but Captain Bisset will not let him bleed out.

"Look!" she shouts.

David glances above their inflatable's rubber hull. What he sees horrifies him.

Huracan's yacht tender hits the rocky ledge and becomes airborne. Its Volvo Penta engine lets out an unearthly howl as it disintegrates. Shards of wood and metal explode across the shore. It's almost impossible to discern anything in the debris cloud, but David sees a mannequin-like figure thrown clear of the wreck. The rag doll bounces and scrapes across the glassy coral, then grazes a boulder and rolls to a stop in the scrubby vegetation.

"You did it!" Sophie shouts.

She slides David into the Zodiac's belly and elevates his legs while compressing his wound. David is confused. Even his vision is failing.

"*No! He's coming around again!*" he cries out in a delirious terror. "*Sophie! Where are you?* Oh god, I've been shot. I hope I'm not ... *dying.*"

"You're going to be okay!"

Sophie looks into his eyes and sees the unmistakable indicators of a man going down. "Huracan's gone. He can't hurt us anymore," she says, her voice breaking as she tries to stay strong. "I'm with you. Help is on its way." She cradles David in her arms, blood dripping through her fingers.

David fights to remain conscious, but finds that time seems to be drifting into the non-linear. Everything is becoming strangely dreamlike, irrelevant. He hears the crack of a pistol. He looks up and sees a flare shooting into the sky.

"Stay awake!" he hears Sophie say.

But her voice seems reverberant and hollow now, barely audible above the ringing in his ears. Even the morning light is fading. It's like a heavy black curtain is being draped over him. It feels *so* comfortable.

"Don't fall asleep, David!" Sophie's voice echoes.

Then, a tornadic whirlwind, helicopter blades, rescue divers, voices. Urgent-sounding voices. Some are familiar. David's thoughts speak to him as a voice inside his head now. *Pong? What are you doing here? Why is Sophie... crying? So tired. Must be what ... dying feels like.*

"Zeke! Daddy's here!" David shouts. Now he's being strapped into something. He's spinning, starting to fly.

"I'm not ready to die!"

"You're not going to die, David" Sophie shouts. Her voice is so far away

So cold. Can't stop shaking. Sophie, don't leave me. Sophie ... don't let me—

Then nothing but a deafening silence within a blinding darkness.

Chapter 42
New Beginnings

An odd whistling noise mixes with a subsonic rumble. The sound is strangely comforting and at the same time familiar. David stirs and a trickle of light washes in as if through a frosted lens. There's a unique smell—of sweat, musty carpet, war, and coffee. Then, the sound of a deep Caribbean voice.

"Good to have you back, young man."

"Tony?"

"*The Lord* was looking over your shoulder," Tony testifies with the cadence of a holy man.

David has no idea where he is, but it feels so safe and warm here, he doesn't want to know. As his eyes unglue, the handsome Bahamian comes into focus. Beside him, a trio of empty intravenous bags hang from a hospital drip stand. David stretches out his hands and toes, relieved that they still seem to be there.

"You're lucky the Rev wasn't using hollowpoints," Tony says. "The bullet went clean through, came out the other side.

Missed your vitals, no broken bones. I put some sutures in and topped you up with two units of AB-negative."

"Trained in field medicine, Tony?"

"Army medic."

"Thanks, Doc."

"Thank Sophie, not me. Without her first aid at sea, well—"

"Sophie?! Where is she? Please tell me she's okay."

"She's shaken up pretty bad, but she'll come out of it. She's been worried sick about you."

David becomes aware of a light pressure on his chest and raises his head to have a look, but there's a sudden tightness around his throat. He reaches up, pulls on a tangled plastic tube, and the whistling sound stops.

"No no. Leave it in," Tony says.

David suddenly realizes how foggy he is. He lets the oxygen tube slip back into place, glances down, and that's when he sees her, lying across his chest, sound asleep. Sophie makes a tired squeak and nuzzles into his chest.

David lifts his head. He recognizes the worn seating and gray interior, and through an oval window, sees a familiar-shaped wing and a turboprop engine.

"Okay if I sit up?"

"If it's okay with her," Tony replies, smiling and motioning at Sophie.

"Nicely done, by the way," the Bahamian adds. "I don't know how you pulled it off."

"Well, even a blind pig finds a truffle now and then," David replies. "Tony, this might sound strange, but unless it's the symptom of a brain injury, I'm pretty sure I smell coffee."

"I thought some fine Colombian might wake you."

"I'd kill for a cup of joe."

"I'll unhook your IV, but you're going to be dizzy, so go easy."

Sophie grumbles as David props himself up. Tony helps her across the plane's aisle, where she collapses into a seat and falls back to sleep. After disconnecting David from the tubes and monitoring devices, Tony watches with a discerning eye as his patient takes his first step toward the cabin front.

"Whoa. A bit wobbly," says David. He stumbles but catches a nearby seat and steadies himself.

Tony grabs him by the arm. "Here. Sit beside Sophie."

"I'm alright, Tony. I can—"

"Sit. That's an order!"

After a blissfully uneventful flight, Sophie and David bid Tony farewell. They deplane onto a section of tarmac at Miami International reserved for military craft. While walking away from the old DC-3 toward the terminal, David notices a mural of a 1940s-style pin-up girl painted on the plane's nose. Above the portrait, a cursive logo reads *Ruthie.*

"Let me guess. Ruthie number three." David says.

"Four, actually," Sophie replies.

"Who is Ruthie?"

"My mom."

David suddenly remembers the story of Ruth Bisset's tragic drowning while she tried to save Sophie's little brother

"What a beautiful woman," David says, admiring her likeness.

"In every way," Sophie replies wistfully. "She was a singer and actress. Met dad when she was touring with the USO. I miss her so much. Not a single day goes by without—" Sophie's voice falters.

"She'd sure be proud of you," David interjects, but Sophie steers the topic into less intrusive territory. She steps back and beams at David, who is now wearing a blue suit, white shirt, black shoes and a thin navy tie.

"Nice homecoming outfit. Dad knows how to pick the clothes."

"No kidding! Who'd believe we spent the last forty-eight hours hanging from the devil's ceiling."

Though outwardly at ease, David is overwhelmed by the intensity of the life experience he's shared with Sophie. He met her barely two days ago, but it feels like he's known her for years. He has no idea what will happen between them as they walk toward a stark mirrored doorway that leads to a glass-and-steel immigration complex.

Will this be where we shake hands and never see each other again? David prays not, but braces himself just in case.

"So, about tonight," Sophie says.

David feels his heart pounding, terrified of becoming the ghost in If You Could Read My Mind, but his worry is hijacked by an annoying beeping sound from his suit pocket. David reaches in and retrieves his pager: Belinda calling. He's amazed that Sophie's team has re-stocked him with his personal items, but simultaneously, the communication device is a reminder of his previous mundane existence, which up until this moment seemed like a lifetime ago.

"That's strange," David says. "It's a garbled message." He pushes on its tiny plastic buttons and reads the text scrolling across the one-inch LCD screen.

"Who is it?" Sophie says as she hands him his passport.

"Belinda," David replies. "My, uh, ex-wife."

There are many words that could describe Sophie's reaction, but thrilled would not be one of them.

"I don't like this," David says as he reads the message.

Sophie leans in for a look.

"What does it say?"

David fumbles with the buttons.

Need you. Hurry. 1475 Industrial Park Rd. Zeke is

Minutes after clearing immigration, Sophie is behind the wheel of her pale blue Mercedes. Once again David is in the passenger seat, this time playing navigator.

"You're sure it's not an old message?" Sophie says as David attempts to pull up a time stamp. Just then, another message beeps in.

Where are you? Please! 1475 Industrial Park Road. Zeke has

Sophie feels her own concern elevating. Something seems off, and they are entering a remote, industrial part of town now. And what David doesn't know, is that Belinda and Zeke spent the last two days in a safe house, after intel revealed a possible threat to them.

"Do you recognize the address?"

"It's a warehouse and office. Belinda did some consulting there, but it was always very hush-hush. I drove her there once and she made me drop her off a block away."

"That's a bit odd."

"It was, but I think she was having an affair with her boss. She got all snippy and evasive whenever I asked her about it. There it is."

David points to a nondescript two story office building. In front of it, a black BMW is angled across two parking spaces. Its rear passenger door is open and the interior dome light is on.

"That's her car."

Sophie pulls over and parks. As they step out and walk up to Belinda's sedan, David sees the base of Zeke's snap-and-go car seat in the back. Lines of worry cloud his face. He looks around, then closes the door.

"This doesn't make any sense," he says.

"We'll figure it out. Come on."

Without another word, they make their way toward the building's entrance. David enters a small reception area and Sophie follows him in, hyperaware of their surroundings.

"Hello!" David shouts. Nothing, until a loud crashing sound resounds from behind a closed door at the end of a hallway. It is followed by a child's voice. Zeke's voice.

"No! Put me down!" he screams.

David bolts toward the door.

"Wait!" Sophie pulls a Glock .22 out of a thigh holster. David eyes bug out when he sees it.

"Take this," she whispers, "and for god's sake, be careful with it."

David flips the safety off. He checks the door handle. It's unlocked.

"Zeke!" David shouts.

"Daddy! I need your help."

David turns to Sophie. Three ... two ... one. They burst through the door into a darkened room.

Overhead lights blaze on, followed by a terrifyingly loud sound.

Chapter 43
Action Diorama

"SURPRISE! Happy birthday to you. Happy birthday to you. Happy birth-day… dear—"

The anthem goes off the rails as partygoers digest the sight of David and Sophie in full combat pose, he with the raised pistol and her in a kung fu stance. They look like theatre lobby action-diorama cutouts. A teary-eyed Zeke runs up to David.

"Daddy! Mom took my truck away."

Belinda is at the front of the group, wearing a pasted-on smile, holding the giant remote-control vehicle. There are balloons and banners everywhere: *Happy Birthday David* and *33 Years Young*.

"This is awkward," Belinda says.

David safeties the gun. A disbelieving smile breaks across his face.

"How long have you been planning this?"

"Long," Belinda replies thinly. She seems frozen, her eyes locked on the mission's engagement ring on Sophie's finger.

"*Oh!*" David says. "Belinda, Sophie. Sophie, Belinda."

People rush up and surround David, mystified as they offer him their well-wishes. Belinda returns the truck to Zeke, who couldn't be happier as he drives it at full speed into the walls.

"We had a great time at Uncle Lindy's, Dad!" Zeke exclaims, "I got to stay up till midnight. You should've come over."

"Good ol' Uncle Lindy, eh?" David says sarcastically. He eyes Belinda.

"Yes, we did have a good time, David. Unfortunately, 'Uncle Lindy' and I had to cancel our night at the Fontainebleau, since Daddy didn't show up for the sleepover."

"I'm so sorry Belinda. You wouldn't believe what happened. I was kidnapped and taken to a tropical island, where there was a nuclear missile and a crazed cult leader who—"

David barely notices a tap on his shoulder, but the sound of a familiar voice stops him cold.

"X! Thanks for making a big party. Many happy birthdays on you."

"Drago?" David turns around and is delighted to see the lanky Slovenian.

"Everybody's at the bar," says Drago. "Come drink off your face. That is how you say, yes?"

"Sure," replies David.

Drago motions for him to follow.

"Oh, David." Belinda smiles wryly. "Go enjoy your party. I can hear all your excuses later."

Just then, a handsome gentleman with salt and pepper hair walks up and reaches for Belinda's hand. David 's eyes widen at the sight, then he follows Drago toward the bar and corrals Sophie along the way. Pong and Tony are there, and so is Ned, who is wearing sunglasses and nursing a coffee at the end of the bar. Beside him, Gilbert is knocking back a rum.

"Good show there, David," Ned says. "Sorry I couldn't have been more help."

"No, it was my fault, Ned. Can't believe I left the damn safety off."

"The fog of war, son. Let's hope we never have to face it again."

David drapes his arm over Sophie's shoulder as the bartender passes them pints.

"To Captain Sophie Bisset," David announces.

He raises his glass and the group join in with a toast in her honor, just as Belinda arrives at the bar with her dashing silver fox in tow. The team bristle when they catch sight of him.

"General Passmore!" Drago exclaims. He and Mr. Pong stand at attention. Ned stays seated, but gives the general a tired salute.

"Hey Lindy," he says.

"At ease, team," General Linden Passmore replies. "You've all performed a great service for humankind, and it is I that salute you." He stands and raises a hand firmly to his forehead.

David uses the moment to slip away with Belinda.

"I don't know where to start," he says. "There's so much to explain. Thanks for doing this. It means more than you could ever know."

"So you were surprised?" Belinda asks.

"Hell yeah! I even forgot it was my birthday!"

"Thank *God!* So, who's the young chick?"

David looks over at Sophie. He can't hide his loving eyes for her.

"You two look good together. I hope it works out," Belinda says.

"And you," David replies, chuckling. "I always knew you dug the older guys, but a general? Not bad." Then the smiles fade. "I'm sorry I screwed up your New Year," David says. "You wouldn't believe me if I told you what I've been through over the last forty-eight hours. I'm having trouble believing it myself. Hopefully someone got in touch with you."

"Thank you for that," Belinda replies. "Yes, they did contact us. That doesn't mean I was happy about it, but things are good now. I've only heard bits and pieces from Linden, but you're some kind of hero around here." She pauses. "But you've always been a hero to that little guy." Belinda points at Zeke.

"Aw, jeez." David says, fighting off a wave of emotion. "Thanks, Belinda. At least we did something right. You know I'll always love you."

"I know," Belinda replies confidently. She turns to the bartender. "How about some music over here!"

The lights dim and the dulcet surf-guitar strains of Santo & Johnny's Sleepwalk start shimmering out of the hall's speaker system.

Sophie rushes over and grabs David by the hand. "Might I have this dance?"

He pulls her in close and they whirl and sway to the music. Feeling Sophie's body pressing into his, David thinks there might just be a future for them. The madness they've been through suddenly feels like it was worth every insane second. They only have eyes for each other as they spin dizzyingly to the melodious guitar tones. Soon the crowd, the lights and even the music fade into the background. David is reminded of something his beloved uncle Jeffrey whispered on his end of days.

"You can never change the past, but you can always change your future. Live life to the fullest, savor every moment, and *never* look back in regret."

EPILOGUE

At a quiet suburban rehabilitation hospital, four figures in surgical gowns huddle over a patient.

"I can't release him. It's only been eight months," Doc Blaine says. "And this is one of the worst cases I've seen." He leans in with a pair of tweezers and tugs at a thin layer of gauze that is covering the patient's face.

"We've finally tamed the infection, but I concur," a female physician adds. "He shouldn't be moved for at least a month, preferably two. I told you people that yesterday. And this CFLS? Never heard of it."

"The Center for Lateral Security is a top-level access program, which is precisely why you haven't heard of us," a tall man replies, his face obscured by a surgical mask. "This patient needs to be in a competent facility. This place is a joke."

The doctors trade a barbed glance as they work on the motionless patient. As the gauze unravels, it grows increasingly crimson in color. The female doctor removes a brace from the patient's left arm, revealing a jagged wound where the radius and ulna bones tore through skin. The patient's hand bears the scars and staple marks of multiple surgeries.

"Let's have a look," Doc Blaine says as he peels off a final layer of gauze. "Very good. The grafts have taken well."

"And he's waking up, right on schedule," the female physician adds. "After eight months in an induced coma."

The patient's visage is a patchy quilt of skin grafts, but a number of features are obvious. The cheekbones are high, the lips thin, and the eyes, as they open, reveal a soft almond shape.

"So, the stories are true?" Doc Blaine queries. "Weapons of mass destruction and such?"

"You know better than to ask," the tall man replies.

"Everyone wants to interrogate this patient, which is out of the question," the female physician adds. "He won't be lucid for weeks. And a metal skewer pierced his larynx and nicked his vocal cord, so he may never speak again."

A short man begins to disconnect the IV lines and reroute them into a battery-powered infusion pump as a voice crackles over a loudspeaker.

"Dr. Marla Shulman, report to triage. Dr. Marla Shulman."

Dr. Shulman walks away from the stretcher. She pulls her surgical mask down.

"For the record, I am not on board with this," she says. "I'm sure Dr. Blaine will agree." She exits into the hospital hallway, where she squeezes past a broad-shouldered man standing outside the door.

Back in the room, the tall man hands Doc Blaine a clipboard. It has an official-looking form attached to it.

"You need to sign this. Now."

Doc Blaine frowns as he snatches the clipboard, then a confused look passes over his face.

"Wait a minute. This is a death certificate."

"Would you prefer if your name was on it?" the short man says. He noses a silenced pistol out from under his scrubs and aims it at the doctor's heart.

Doc Blaine is without words. He glances at a red emergency-alert button on the wall.

"Don't even think about it," the gunman says. "This is a simple equation. You sign it, you live."

The tall man takes off his surgical outfit, and he's wearing a finely tailored black suit and tie under it. His mask comes off, uncovering a hollow cheeked face. It is Aaden—the man who switched computer bags with Sophie at the bus stop, and who was last seen shot and apparently "killed" at the Greater God temple.

"I can't sign this," Dr. Blaine says. "It goes against everythi—"

"Enough!" The short man tears off his scrubs and throws them to the floor. He too is dressed in an expensive suit, and has a moustache and thin goatee. This man is Ennio, the slippery Russian agent.

Ennio walks to the door and bangs on it. The barrel-chested individual from the hallway enters, wheeling a massive wooden casket in front of him that barely fits through the door.

"Audrius has a present for you," Ennio says.

Doc Blaine lunges for the emergency button, but Aaden pounces on him and wraps an elbow around his neck. He jams his other arm behind it. Blaine tries to speak, but only gurgling sounds sputter out of his mouth. Audrius shuts the door and locks it, then saunters up to the doctor, stopping inches away from him. He reaches into his jacket, pulls out an envelope and eyes him coldly as he holds it up.

"Take it," Aaden says. "Do you think you can do that?"

Dr. Blaine nods.

"And you're not going to try anything stupid if I let you go?"

Blaine shakes his head.

Aaden releases his grip and the doctor gasps for air. Ennio holsters the pistol inside his suit jacket, then pulls out a decorative handkerchief and tucks it into his breast pocket. Doc Blaine takes the envelope from Audrius.

"There's a card in the envelope with account information on it," Ennio says as he finesses the handkerchief into a fashionable triangular shape. "Five hundred thousand dollars, in an untraceable offshore fund. Think of it as a signing bonus, or college tuition for those beautiful sons of yours."

Audrius holds up a picture of Doc Blaine with his wife and two boys on a tropical beach.

"All you have to do is put your signature on the page."

"Or, you can leave here in that wooden box," Aaden adds.

"And if I sign? You people will leave me alone?" the doctor asks, hiding his fury as he snatches the envelope from Audrius.

"That depends," Aaden replies. "You left the room when you heard the explosion."

Blaine looks confused.

"When you returned, the patient was gone. Make no mention of the death certificate. Now sign it. Before I change my mind!"

"Okay. I'll sign. But please— no family involvement."

With a shaky hand, Doc Blaine reaches for a pen at the top of the clipboard.

"That is entirely up to you," Ennio says. He retrieves what looks like a tiny radio transmitter from inside his suit pocket. He raises its antenna and flips a switch at the top, causing a circular button to glow red.

Dr. Blaine, faced with the choice of silver or lead, endorses the document. Aaden snatches the paper from him and stuffs it into his jacket pocket, then glances at Ennio and gives him a purposeful nod. Ennio presses down on the electronic device's button. Simultaneously, a window-shaking concussion reports from outside the hospital, followed by the sound of glass breaking and car alarms beeping. An alarm erupts in the hospital as a voice blasts out of loudspeakers.

"Attention. This is a Code Red. Emergency services are on route. Stay where you are and await further instructions. Attention. This is a Code Red..."

"There's one more thing, Doctor Blaine," Aaden says as Audrius lifts the coffin's lid. "You need to help us get the patient into the casket. Then, you're free to go. But remember what I told you, and do not deviate from the story. Understand?"

Doc Blaine recites his lines. "I heard the explosion, ran to see what it was. When I returned, the patient was gone."

The four men lift the body into the box. Huracan protests with frightened grunts as he slides into it, but Ennio speaks to him gently.

"It's okay, Reverend. We're getting you out of here."

Ennio places a translucent oxygen mask over Huracan's nose and mouth. He lays the portable IV pump on his chest and turns a light on inside the casket, before Audrius shuts the lid and ratchets it into place.

"Time for you to go now, Doctor," Aaden says. "Make sure that no one comes this way for ten minutes. Understand?"

"Understood."

Blaine exits into the hallway. Though plagued with guilt, the thought of a $500,000 slush fund puts a wry smile on the doctor's face, the smile of a man who has just cheated the hangman's noose.

In the corridor, staff members are scurrying about as they lock the hospital down. A hundred feet away, a cloud of oily gray smoke is billowing out of the central lobby.

Audrius rolls the casket out of the room with Ennio behind him. Aaden, wearing aviator sunglasses, leads them with the signed certificate in hand. They approach a sliding glass door that exits into the parking lot, where a frantic-looking security guard is shouting into a walkie-talkie. Outside, a crescendo of sirens are blaring. A voice crackles over the officer's radio:

"This is Rescue One. We are proceeding to the east lot. Ensure the roadway is unobstructed, and that all civilians and unnecessary personnel are cleared from the area."

"Roger that, Rescue One," the security officer replies into her walkie-talkie. "There is a car on fire in J-sector. Will ensure that your pathway is clear. Also, we have smoke in the central atrium, I repeat, smoke in the central atrium."

"Copy that. Arriving now."

Aaden shows the death certificate to the security guard, but she waves him past, too distracted to notice muffled thuds coming from the casket.

Outside, on a freshly paved parking loop, a black hearse awaits them. Brutus is standing at the rear of the Lucky Tiger Funeral Home vehicle.

He swings the tailgate open, and together with Audrius, they hook the casket onto the vehicle's loading mechanism. Within seconds, it is inside the hearse. Ennio walks up to Aaden.

"That was almost too easy," he says, half smirking.

"We need to leave here. Pronto," Aaden replies.

Ennio's cockiness suddenly fades.

"Listen—I have to say ... I'm sorry about your brother."

"It wasn't your call. You had to do it."

"I know, but you two—twins and all?! If that asshole David Wesson hadn't gone all Johnny Boy Scout and followed him to the church like a lost puppy dog, your brother would still be—"

"Enough! You got the order, you carried it out. Case closed. The whole operation was a giant fuckup. This will be the last you ever speak of it."

"So you don't hold me responsible for his dea—"

"Bring Wesson to me."

"Consider it done, Colonel Smirnov," Ennio says. "See you at the airfield. Wheels-up at 1300."

"We'll be there."

Ennio clambers into the back of the hearse and Brutus shuts the door behind him.

As they accelerate out of the parking loop toward the exit, first responder vehicles are arriving from all directions. Ennio flips a metal clasp on the side of the funeral box and raises the lid. Inside the white padded casing, Huracan's eyes dart nervously.

"You're with us now, Reverend," Ennio says. "We're bringing you to your new kingdom."

Huracan responds with an animalistic moan, the only sound he can produce through splintered vocal cords.

"Shhh, lord," Ennio whispers softly. "Your flock awaits you. Such cruel injustice shall be repaid. In tenfold. Soon, you shall have what we all crave more than anything. Revenge!"

Huracan's grafted face contorts and his eyes jolt open. His facial skin stretches and his cracked lips part, revealing angry clenched teeth. It's like gazing upon the megalithic stone face of the Mayan god Juracán, from whom the Reverend created his namesake. His body starts convulsing as he raises his mangled hand.

Huracan's fingers clench together, forming a gnarled fist. One of the grafts tears away, revealing the white glare of bone beneath the dermis. Blood seeps across his skeletal hand and a hollow growl rattles out of the Reverend's chest.

Ennio leans in close to him.

"Do not fret, wondrous lord," he says, tears welling in his eyes as he brushes Huracan's brow lovingly. "Your sun shall soon rise again."

The End

An Emmy Award-winning songwriter, musician, composer and producer with 30+ years of experience, Toronto-based Anthony Vanderburgh has been called upon for his musical skills by prominent artists, networks and record companies.

His producing work with Dan Hill helped garner the Canadian songwriting legend a number of hit covers for artists as varied as Celine Dion and The Backstreet Boys. Vanderburgh also helped launch the careers of adult-contemporary singer Amy Sky, Juno Award winning metal group Slik Toxik (Hard Rock Album of the Year1993), and Chicago's singer Neil Donell. His work with Sky earned two Top 5 singles, and writing for Donell led to a Top 5 hit.

As a guitarist, Vanderburgh toured extensively with acts such as Roch Voisine, Dan Hill, Alan Frew (of Glass Tiger), and numerous Top 40 bands dating back to the eighties. He has recorded in Los Angeles, Frankfurt and Nashville.

Vanderburgh has composed soundtracks for over 200 episodes of television. He received a 2009 Emmy Award for his co-written theme song to the animated series 6teen. He has been honored with other awards, including SOCAN's Top International (and Domestic) Television Series for his composing on 6teen in 2010 and, more recently, an Alumni of Distinction from Humber College of Creative Arts and a Premiere's Award nomination.

During a long-overdue hiatus from music, Vanderburgh has refocused his creative energies on writing his own narratives, and is excited to have completed his first novel, an adventure-thriller entitled, 'Careful What You Die For'.

Regarding the experience of writing his first book, Vanderburgh says, "Writing a novel is like composing a symphony. Every character is an instrument with their own unique voice, timbre and melodic arc. How these characters are juxtaposed and the ways in which they interact, in both harmony and dissonance, creates an ensemble of powerful and sometimes beautiful music."

www.ingramcontent.com/pod-product-compliance
Lightning Source LLC
Chambersburg PA
CBHW070116120726
47909CB00002B/614